NOEL

STAY ANOTHER DAY

TISHA ANDREWS

SYNOPSIS

Noel Lancaster has been in love with her male best friend, Desmond McBride, forever. They have been glued to the hips as kids only for Desmond to make the hugest mistake of his life, severing the trust and ties they once held. While Desmond chooses to spend the holidays with his love, Noel decides to spend it in Mason with her niece and nephew in tow.

Knight Commodore, prestigious millionaire with a not so happy childhood, despises holidays. He'd rather others enjoy it with their families while he struggles to just get through them one holiday at a time. Unfortunately for him, sister Queen has other plans when she suggests they spend this year's Christmas together in Mason with hopes of their family growing closer.

Knight compromises and gives in but asks that he has

some time alone before they come together as a family. Especially when Rayelle, a woman he's known almost all of his life, reminds him why he can't let his guard down to trust or love a woman.

When he does, his path crosses with the likes of Noel and the ride takes off hard and fast when they both find a way to turn their personal and family misfortune into a reason to forgive and love.

PREFACE

Happy Holidays, Readers, new and old!

I am so excited to have penned my third holiday story and even more excited that I get to share it with you. The beauty of this one is my introduction of new characters that I pray you get a chance to fall in love with the way that I have.

Having said that, please know that this story is not a full-length novel, but it is full of drama, betrayal, some sexual tension and finally, love. An insta-love, too!

That means the ride will be fast but relatable as to why my hero and heroine find each other and make a connection early on in their quest of healing from pain while opening up themselves to give and receive love.

My stories are penned with a focus on a redemptive love. That means the characters are flawed, making poor choices either intentionally or unintentionally, yet need a healthy love to get to a good place in their life. Or they are scarred from those around them or situations they have been placed in, hardening their hearts.

If you can rock with that and experience this journey the way that Knight and Noel gave it to me, keep reading! And when you are done reading, please be so kind as to leave me an honest review.

They make me better. On that note, let's do this!

1

NOEL LANCASTER

"I DON'T UNDERSTAND WHY I STILL HAVE TO GO, THOUGH," I grumbled lowly, looking at my best friend, Desmond. "Everyone going has someone but me," I said, then gave my father a tight-lipped smile when he glared my way. For years, the Lancasters as a family spent Christmas in the family's cabin in Mason, a small town in the mountains just north of our hometown, Jonestown.

My grandfather, may God rest his soul, left it to my parents as a part of his will when we were just kids. Over the years, the use of it changed from romantic getaways my sister, Nyla, had with her husband, Payne, to my brother hanging out with his college roommates as a boys' trip. But the one thing that remained a constant was us going as a family during the holidays for Christmas.

Unfortunately, this year, my father wanted to stay back in

Jonestown with my mother running the family pet store and kennel. He claimed he had lots of orders coming in around the holiday time and the money was just too good to leave on the table. That meant taking advantage of impulsive and last-minute shoppers. As for the kennel, that was ran by my Uncle Kenny. Unlike my father, Uncle Kenny seemed eager to kick up his feet at home so he could eat and go watch sports on Christmas day. He already had a rotation of college part-timers for his side of the business, eager to hustle up money over the holiday break.

Since I was little, Uncle Kenny was always the one who took life a little less serious. He didn't stress or commit to much of anything that didn't suit his lifestyle, which was modest with no children and two dogs at home. So, it was no surprise that while they owned it jointly as brothers, my father was the one to take on the lead and ultimately, the load to keep things running smoothly.

"The kids will be there, too, Noel. I don't understand what the problem is. They adore you and they will keep you pretty busy. I'm just saying," my mother said as Nyla sighed, knowing exactly why I felt the way that I did. She was the only one who knew my entire being belonged to Desmond McBride since I was like ten. We just sort of friend zoned each other until Desmond's elaborate plans came into fruition after getting his masters this summer in electrical engineering.

While I had a college degree in business myself, my

father only paid for what student aid didn't cover just so I could do what I was doing now. That's working for the family business. Desmond told me to just hold on. He had dreams and those dreams included his best friend, the one he vowed to love forever, begging me to hold on and be patient before we made things official.

I just didn't know holding on meant him securing a girlfriend in the process. We really hadn't been on the best terms, when after six months, he shows up to the pet store with *her*. Her being his girlfriend, Cassidy.

He gave me some story about why they were hanging out, that they had met on campus and had studied together over the summer. But not Miss Cassidy. Oh no, she spared nothing. He was out here courting her across town, knowing I wouldn't see a thing since all I did was what I was doing when they both showed up—working. She even had me beating the aisles, looking for things for Neechie, her pet Chihuahua.

Once I saw her and the way he carried on like he was in love, I couldn't help but understand. Why choose me, the plain old, tomboy best friend who'd rather hike, ski or hunt game when you can have the next Miss America who smiled like the cameras were snapping as she whipped her hair back and forth?

"And I adore them. You all know that," I replied, stirring my food around on the plate. "It's just..."

"It's just Noel just being a baby. But it's my fault,"

Desmond spoke up, as if that would make me feel any better. "I had something come up this year that I just couldn't move around."

"Oh, yeah?" my brother, Neil, chimed in, eyeing him suspiciously. "Well, if it's your girlfriend, I'm glad you're finally admitting that. I've been told you two that this, whatever you two have, is crazy. No chick wants her man all booed up with his *female* best friend for the holiday. It's just not natural."

"I'm sorry, but I am sitting here," I said, as Nyla grabbed my hand, rubbing it. "And she's not his girlfriend. She's just a friend."

"A friend he's most definitely smashing," Neil countered as Desmond's eyes bucked.

"Look, Nollie," my father said, calling me by my nickname as he warned Neil with a look to cut it out. "Maybe we can close the store and come along. Besides, the cabin is large enough and there is plenty of space if you do want to bring someone besides Desmond," he said, as Desmond whipped his head my way.

A light snicker from Neil didn't go unnoticed followed by a blunt thump underneath the table, which I knew was a kick from Nyla against Neil's leg for him to cut it out.

"Noel, you have a boyfriend?" my mother probed excitedly.

"Of course not," I countered quickly, totally embarrassed while my niece, Paige, giggled. I swear she was almost seven going on sixteen, acting like her mother. What did she know about boyfriends? Payne Junior or PJ, my nephew who was four, looked around unenthused. He couldn't care less about our grown-up problems, eager to get back to *Paw Patrol*.

"Actually, since there is enough room, I was thinking that maybe I can bring Cassidy," Desmond eased in, dropping a huge ass bomb on us. "I mean, since Noel might have a boyfriend."

What the fuck? How did this all turn into me having a boyfriend? I could kill them all right now. Every single one of them. Well, except Nyla and the kids. Her husband Payne could go, too, since he cosigned everything Neil did or said. I wasn't surprised, though, since they were best friends before he and Nyla got married.

"Those plans changed that quickly, huh, bro?" Neil instigated, shaking his head as he gave me that look of *I told you so.* "This is going to get very interesting," he mumbled when I heard another kick. "Would you stop that?" he whispered forcefully under his breath at Nyla.

"I don't see why not," my father said with a shrug. "Since you and Nollie aren't going to the next level, she should bring her boyfriend."

"Dang, Pops. You're a savage," Neil said, while Nyla snorted, holding her belly. I'm glad this was comical to them while I sat here, struggling not to fall apart. I was in tears, looking for my mother to save me. I had no boyfriend while Desmond sat here and tried to play me in front of my family.

Payne stood up and cleared his throat, which thankfully, he did to get all of the attention off of me. Desmond was pissed and so was I. Especially since he started all of this once my parents mentioned they weren't coming up to Mason this year. He instantly remembered his plans, laying them on me in front of everyone. So fucking sway. Cryptic plans, too, since this scheduling conflict had no details.

"Well, since everyone's focused on what we are doing for Christmas, this seems like a good time to make another announcement."

"Oh, I like announcements," my mother egged on while Desmond tried to grab my hand before I snatched it away.

"I'm glad you do, Mom," Payne said, taking a deep breath. "I have something different planned for the misses and I," he said, smiling as he lowered himself down to one knee.

A gasp escaped Nyla's mouth, along with my mother's while Neil and my father slapped five, celebrating a proposal, I suppose. They were already married, but with men, who knows why they do the things they do. Then I recalled the first proposal the day of Nyla's college graduation. The graduation that occurred just seven months before Paige's birth, but who's counting, right? Yet and still, Nyla chose right by saying yes, and here they were, basking in their love for each other as he looked at her with loving eyes.

"Nyla Elizabeth Wyndham, would you do me the honor of being my wife *again*?" he asked as my mother squealed. You would have thought he had proposed to her. My father gave her a look, shaking his head as she began to cry. He wouldn't understand anyway. My father, that is, since my mother waited on him hand and foot. That further confirmed I was in a room with men full of themselves.

"Yes!" Paige screamed, answering for her mother while PJ groaned and asked if he could get up now.

Even though I wanted to really cry, dabbing my eyes quickly while they all cheered, I decided to be happy for my sister. She worked just as hard at the store as I did, although mostly keeping the books while I worked the floor. Neil was over inventory, which was good since he wasn't the most pleasant person to deal with. That was where I came in, being the engaging, sometimes goofy one who made others feel good about not knowing a thing about why they wanted a pet or what to buy for them if they did get one.

"Oh, baby. Of course, I will," she cooed, poking her lips out as he pecked them while sliding her ring on.

All this meant was I was really spending Christmas with the kids, Cookie, who was the family's Labrador, Neil and his girlfriend, Erin, and maybe Desmond and his new friend, if he dared to push his outlandish agenda being childish.

Great. Just fucking great.

"Hey," Nyla said to me lowly, motioning for me to follow her to the kitchen. I took a deep breath and stood, hoping we wouldn't get fussed at for getting up. I doubted that, though, since all the men were congratulating Payne. "Are you going to be okay?" she whispered, looking over my shoulder, I'm sure at Desmond.

"Of course, I will, Nyla," I smiled and lied, eyeing her yellow canary wedding ring she'd only wanted since forever.

Yellow was her favorite color while mine was a cinnamon, sort of the complexion of my skin. I don't know if my husband, wherever he may be in the universe, would go for that as a ring color, but I wasn't holding my breath about it, either. Not when I looked like a boy on most days with golden dread locs for easy upkeep. Especially when it came to hiking, shooting game in the forest or skiing in the mountains. I was told I was a natural over the years and I really was. It was my getaway from my day-to-day life when I did get a chance to do it with Desmond after being swamped down with work.

Don't get me wrong, I loved what we did and represented to the community. A few years back, we were able to work with law enforcement by offering rescue dogs as a way to give back. I wanted to sign us up for the program where some of our dogs could become companions for emotional support for people struggling with mental health issues. But none of that made me not want Desmond, and now sadly, I wanted him even more.

"He's a dick, you know," she said, referring to Desmond. "I actually am glad he has a girlfriend, Noel."

"Friend," I corrected her. "She's just a friend."

"Fine, Noel. *Just a friend.* One he is trying to take to

Mason since plans just miraculously changed. I'm sorry, but he's been blocking for years. Especially after he got you to... you know what," she whispered, leaning in closer to me.

"Nope, nope. We are not going there," I reminded her, speaking of when I gave my virginity to him. If we did, I'd be snotting all over the place as I quickly fanned my face and blinked my eyes, fighting back the tears.

"I'm just saying..." she said, sighing. "I like him, and I get why you do, too, but maybe it's time to give it up, sis. Tell him he can't bring this so-called friend. We are not that friendly, and you deserve better. After you do, peace out to his blocking ass," she told me as we heard our father call out to us.

"Coming, Daddy!" I replied. "Bringing the dessert," I lied, but had to since they'd be expecting it. "I guess we survived another Thanksgiving dinner," I said, giving her a hug. "Thanks, Nyla. And I'm sorry about earlier."

"No apology needed. We all work hard at the store, but no one harder than you. You deserve some time off. Matter of fact, once we all get back from the holidays, maybe we create a new tradition. Especially since you will have a man by then," she sassed, grabbing the sweet potato pie off the counter while I grabbed the ice cream.

"Oh, God. Would you all stop it," I groaned.

"I'm just saying, maybe Mason has something or someone waiting for you," she said, grinning mischievously. "Stop underestimating yourself. What Desmond is taking for granted, some other man just may not, Nollie. Go out when you get there, hit up the lounge and sing karaoke, dance and live a little. Hey, maybe a one-night stand."

"A one-night stand? Nyla, you're going too far."

"I'm just saying, live in the moment and not in your head."

"Well, I'd have to actually attract another man for that to happen," I told her as we headed by to the dining area. "Have you looked at me?"

"Stop that," she whispered, then smiled as we presented the pie and ice cream.

As we did, Desmond barely looked my way, already knowing I was upset. All these mixed messages the past six months was for the birds, but he sent a clear one tonight and we were done. All I would have is memories, most of them with him playing with my heart the more I reminisced.

"Come here," he said, taking me by my hand. Butterflies danced around in my belly instantly as he gave me that smile, the one where his lip curled slightly to the left. It was a mischievous one; one that told what he was thinking and nothing nice. Yes, God.

He wanted to be close to me. I needed him to be close to me. So, I obliged him as I fell in line, as our walk slowed down now to a crawl.

This was us, Noel and Desmond, when no one was around. We were more than best friends. We actually emotionally connected, chained down at our souls with the most kick ass chem-

istry. It was insane. Yet publicly, he wouldn't show it. He refused to show it and I let that bullshit slide.

"I like your hair like that," he said, smiling as he kicked a few rocks on the ground. "You're letting it grow. You know how I like to mess that shit up."

"Ugh, and you know how I hate when you do," I replied, tucking my lips. I fought hard to cease the smile that was threatening to form as he rubbed the top of my hand with the pad of his thumb. My center thumped and he knew it, too. He was the only man to know.

"I know what you don't hate, though," he said, his voice low and layered with hints of lust as he stopped us from walking.

"What?" I replied, daring not to look his way as I dropped my eyes. I feared looking in them, losing myself.

Whenever Desmond got like this, I was powerless. I was no longer the best friend, the tomboy I had naturally grew up to be. The one that liked being tough, taking hits and getting up with ease during any sport or rough play. I was like the little girl melting in front of her lifetime crush, the one that controlled the cadence of her heartbeat and every breath she needed to take.

"Me" he eased in between the sounds of leaves that lifted by the air as he leaned down and pressed his lips against mine. It felt right, so right, as if that's where his lips were supposed to be. I mirrored the motions of his mouth and when he slightly parted my lips, I allowed his tongue to slip inside my mouth.

I groaned.

He moaned.

He took my neck.

I tugged on his shirt.

It was the dance of two best friends, hiding in plain sight, loving on each other only for it to be snatched away when he pulled back, ending the kiss. His forehead, however, rested against mine with his eyes closed. I silently begged him to be mine, panting as I fought to catch my breath.

"I love you, Noel, and only you but..."

Please, no. It's happening again. I already knew the drill, the excuses, the reasons why we couldn't be together now. He was about to say that we were "forever best friends" who had a goal. And while the term in and of itself was endearing, it made me feel as if I was holding my breath day in and day out since it was him that had the goal. I just wanted to be his. I didn't care about some elaborate lifestyle. Besides, even broke my heart would still only want one man—Desmond McBride.

"I know," I said, tucking my lips where my tongue was met with the taste of Spearmint gum from his mouth. A taste I wished I could taste forever.

Ugh, I hated him. I swear I do. I needed more. I needed him and I needed him now.

2

NOEL LANCASTER

After dinner was over and all the dishes were washed and put away, Desmond was sitting in the living room. He even had his feet perched up on the coffee table, ready to watch Thanksgiving Day football with Neil and Payne. He looked happy, so happy, as if this was right where he belonged. My heart knew he was playing me. Cassidy had won, whatever that meant. He was her problem now. Not mine yet you couldn't tell as he sat like the perfect fixture that was there just for me.

"I have my own announcement to make, too," I said, standing in the doorway of the living room with my shoulders pushed back. As I stared directly at Desmond, my hands became clammy and I started to shake. So much for those damn shoulders being pushed back. I was mentally a mess.

It was now or never as Nyla whispered behind my back, "You can do it. Send his bitch ass on his way, sis."

"Desmond?" I called out to him with my eyes pinched tightly. *You will not cry in front of this piece of shit, Noel. You will not.* When I opened my eyes, they landed where they always had since I was ten as his warm, penny-colored eyes soaked me up, forcing me to drop my head.

If I looked at him anymore, I wouldn't have the courage to reject this beautiful man, skin the color of light maple syrup with full lips. Kissable lips I could feel even now all over mine. Still, stolen moments were no longer enough as he called out my name and I somehow regained my strength.

"Yes, Noel?" he said. Oh, shit. I hated the way he said my name, the sound of it rolling off of his tongue coupled with nervousness.

He was wearing me down and not even trying. He was just being him, the same ten-year-old boy that stole my heart. I could always tell when he was nervous, just like now as he twisted his lip to the left and chewed on the inside of his jaw.

"Bitch, do it," Nyla whispered, crotched down behind the wall in the kitchen. My sister is fucking nuts, but hey, so am I. I'm getting dumped for the holidays while dude was chilling in my family like it was okay.

"Really, Noel? We're about to watch the game. You two just sat next to each other for freaking two hours. What could you possibly want to talk about right before the kick-off? Just date already and have him ditch old girl so you two can stop annoying me," Neil scoffed.

"Fine," I said with clenched fists. "Desmond, it's over. We are done. And no, you cannot bring your damn girlfriend, friend, or whoever she is to Mason with us. You chose, so now I am choosing. I can't and I won't do this thing between us anymore."

"Wow," Payne said, chuckling lowly under his breath. "Nyla has to be here for this," he said as he smiled, fishing his cell out of his pocket. Too bad he didn't know her silly butt was on the floor with her eyes bucked, silently screaming. "Epic." He chuckled.

"It's about damn time," Neil chimed in, grinning. "D, man. Raise up out of here. You heard her."

"Wh—what?" He laughed, sitting up and staring at me.

His skin flushed as his jaw twitched even more as if I'd spoken some kind of language he needed to be translated for him.

"What do you mean it's over? Us? Over?" he asked, laughing more so to himself as if I'd told a joke. "You can't be serious, Nollie. Come here...please," he said, waving me over with his hand.

"No," I told him, although just barely the longer he pleaded with me with his eyes. His fucking eyes that were like maple magnets of love. I was fucked. Somebody needed to step in and save me and fast.

"Des, man. The shit's simple to me. She said you two are done. You need help getting out that door?" Neil offered.

The last person Desmond would go up against was Neil, who had been waiting for years to kick his ass. Payne was trained to go, who would eagerly help him, yet was the calmer one out of the two of them as he told Neil to chill.

"Noel, I love you. I'm *in love* with you, but we've talked about this, right? The plan, Nollie. The fucking plan."

"We have, and talking time is over."

"Wow." He laughed, staring at me in disbelief. "Alright then," he mumbled, getting up as he looked my way. "I'll give you some space, but don't forget about us, Nollie. Everything about me is because of you, my forever best friend."

"This shit's so corny," Neil scoffed. "My forever best friend," he said, mocking him. "Forever just ended, fuck boy."

Once the door closed and I heard it click, I fucking cried. I literally cried. What was I going to do without Desmond McBride?

I'd only loved him more than half of my life. Now I had nothing to look forward to when it came to love. Absolutely nothing.

3

KNIGHT COMMODORE

"NOPE, PUT THAT AWAY," QUEEN SAID TO ME, STARING DOWN at my cellphone. "We have one rule during meal time, and what's that, Malachi?" my sister asked her pussy-whipped husband.

I love Malachi for real for being a solid dude when it came to Queen, but I wished he used at least one of his balls or asked to borrow it so he could check her sometimes. He was more worred about Queen's little bossy ass than the damage King or I could do. Trust me on this. A whipped cupcake.

Sometimes I had to remind her that not only was I her brother and the oldest, but that she worked for me. The only people that had to take orders from her were the ones who actually lived with her, which included my niece and nephew.

When I heard snickering from King, I shot his ass a look since I employed him, too. My days of hitting up corner stores late night or garbage bins first thing in the morning before the grocery store opened were a thing of the past.

I went from despising the sun rising to beating the sun rising being the founder and CEO of Commodore Enterprises or CE for short. I had put my entire family on and a few from around the way I'd met in foster care like Rayelle who was sort of my situation and my boy Stephen. He wasn't an executive, but I made sure Queen went out and found him and now he was head of our security.

We somehow took advantage of that free state tuition after being wards of the state and now we practically ran the world. What started out as me working at a debt collection agency buying bad debt and recouping double, sometimes triple that, became a passion of mine.

Numbers were simple like black and white, and easy to manipulate. In no time, I caught on to how one credit card in college could ruin your credit and spending power for life. I saw both sides of it, though, being a victim of the system myself. But when a motherfucker was just living reckless or impulsive when it came to how they spent their money, that's where CE came in. I'd bail them out and resell the debt, or better yet, buy their fucking company.

I wasn't totally heartless, though, since I made sure CE was a staple in the community, giving back to businesses and the citizens of Jonestown. Most times anonymously. I didn't want the clout that came with writing a check, sometimes a blank one when I allowed King to fill it out. See, I trusted no one except King and Queen. And what King couldn't handle, Queen came in like the bulldozing beast she was and handled all of our legal affairs.

Everyone in the family was eating off the table at CE. Even Cleo, although I kept her ass as far from me as possible. I didn't have a mother. I lost mine, so she had to be something else to me, and right now, I didn't even know what that was except what she had always been: a bill and a liability.

She was well provided for with a ten thousand dollar a month stipend to do whatever the hell she wanted, which was fine by me. My only requirement was that she stayed committed to being clean and sober, attended her meetings and stopped begging to be in my life.

She didn't deserve my love, so fuck her.

"I tell him all the time he works way too much, girl. But..." was all Rayelle said as I looked her way, shutting her commentary down. She didn't have to tell me anything. The money I made provided for the lifestyle they all lived. Including Rayelle and her shady-ass family. Especially her convict of a brother, Raynard, who was a dumb ass jack boy who traded group homes for prison.

Rayelle came with her own shit, too, that I let slide because, believe it or not, her compassion that day many years ago in the form of a Nintendo, gave her a little space in my life. Never my heart, but I fucked with her. Stayed in touch with her when I left the group home and returned back to Cleo with my siblings at seventeen.

I was close to knocking on adulthood's door when the counselor and the judge told us we were going home. Home? Hmph, I wasn't sure what that was, but it was better than being separated from Queen and King. And once Rayelle knew how to find me, she became a small fixture in my life that somewhat kept the beast at bay.

Nothing serious to me. Fucking mostly and getting money, but let Rayelle tell it, she was going to be the one and only Mrs. Knight Commodore. So much for women residing in the heads who'd bitten off more than they could chew. That was Rayelle. She could show up to CE with heels on and kill the boardroom but be on her knees by lunchtime under my desk, sucking me off. That was our reality, yet here she was with me at my family's Thanksigiving dinner instead of spending it with her own.

"It's Thanksgiving, Knight. That's all I'm saying," Rayelle huffed lowly, her slanted green eyes turning like glass as they became misty. I learned that was her go-to method to get me to succumb to some bullshit.

It was like a switch that she could flip on and off, glamouring others to do what she wanted them to do, but not with me. That only hardened my heart even more. I hated a bullshitter and a manipulator, falling victim to Cleo's antics most of my life. That was a trigger and Rayelle knew it who still tried her hand with me in front of Queen, who was very observant.

"That's enough, Rayelle. It's fine," Queen intervened. "As long as he puts it away now," she said as I slid my cell into my pocket. "Thank you, Knight. So nice of you to join us."

"Yeah," was all I said, laughing but not out of humor. Sadly, Rayelle felt that earned her some points in Queen's eyes who knew I gave no fucks about her. In fact, Rayelle knew that Queen was the only woman who could make me do something as she sat there and smirked, stabbing a piece of honey baked ham.

"Guess it takes the power of Queen to save the day," she muttered just loud enough for everyone to hear when Queen dropped her fork.

"Seriously, Rayelle?"

"Hey, hey. It's Thanksgiving, ladies," Malachi said, easing over and kissing Queen on the cheek as she shot daggers with her eyes Rayelle's way. "It's a time to reflect and think of reasons we are grateful."

"I'll be grateful when Knight informs his staff that family dinner means just that. Family," Queen slid in while King hollered, clapping his hands.

"Sis, you're cold, baby girl. Chill," he said while his space cadet girlfriend, Racha, grinned nervously. That's all Racha did was grin and wave like she was on the fucking runway. She was an Instagram model from Ethiopia who rarely spoke, but if King loved it, I didn't give a shit he he chose to lay up with a mute.

"Knight?" Rayelle said, tossing her napkin on the table as she lifted a brow. I wasn't sure what she expected me to do. She had already knew what was up, but since she forced my hand, I had to oblige her.

"Let me walk you to the door," I whispered in her ear, my eyes affixed on Queen, who was clearly unraveling. Queen couldn't fight for shit, but she didn't have to.That was my job and always had been. So it was my job to remove the problem out of the equation.

"What?" Rayelle snapped, sucking her teeth. "Dinner is not over."

"See, it is for you," Queen said, winking her eye, with her instigating behind.

"What about Racha?" she countered, leaning forward and towards her and King.

"Aye, hold up now. Knight, put a leash on your pet. Don't worry about mine. She's trained and ready to go," this nutcase said while Racha's exotic, penny-colored eyes turned dark. Hell, maybe that's why he had her around. Probably practicing hoodoo on Rayelle without even saying a word.

"Get your purse," I insisted lowly, taking her firmly by her forearm. I was trying not to cause a scene with my niece and nephew there, but they were tuned in, chewing like little horses.

"See you around, Rayellle," Mallory, Queen's daugther, sang while Malachi shushed her.

"What about the Miss?" MJ asked, realizing what Mallory said.

"Oh, she's going to *miss* a lot. Especially the trip I have planned for the Commodor family in Mason. Goodbye, girl. Get you a life and one that does not include me and my family. Checkmate."

I guess you figured it out by now that we were all named after chess pieces on a chess board. My father, Lester, loved to play chess. He said it was empowering, made a man think and think some more before he did something stupid and fucked his life up. I suppose that did apply to how he moved, but one wrong move after a traffic stop resulted in one bullet to the chest that took his life.

My father had an outstanding warrant, and before he could even fathom being away from Cleo, he tried to take off, hit a fire extinguiser and his car flipped over. If that was love, they could keep it. My mother, to this day, won't go down that street, but I would. It reminded me that no feelings and self control were the only true tools to generate success. Because an angry Knight Commodore was a dangerous one. I refused to be that and risk leaving my family behind.

"What's up with all this talk about Mason?" I asked her once Rayelle left without further incident. I was going to handle that later in private, but for now, Queen was really showing her ass today.

"Mason. M-A-S-O-N. Mason."

"Get your wife, Mal," I told him, easing down in my chair. She was on one today, but she'd better calm down.

"Oh, lighten up. You didn't want her here anyway," she chortled, scooping up a spoonful of her infamous seven cheese macaroni and cheese. I didn't, but still. It was hard for me to sit around a dinner table already. We barely did it as children, and after fighting so much in the group home, I mostly ate meals alone.

"Queen?" I said to her sternly, looking at the kids.

"What? They know she's not family," she said dismissively while MJ asked was that my girlfriend. What did he know about a girlfriend at four?

"No, she's not," Queen answered for me. "And she's also not going to Mason. Besides it being the town of magic and love, I heard there might be a few cabins or plots to build some cabins on. Imagine CE taking over in Mason."

"And why would I want to have my hand in anything affilitated with magic and love, Queen?" I asked with furrowed brows when she looked King's way. That alone told me he was already in on it.

"Easily six million a year if we bought a lot of them and that's just seasonal rental alone. Or better yet, find out who owns them and are behind on their mortages. That way, we are being benelovent financing low-rate loans while making a little money," King spoke effortlessly like the chief financial officer I had groomed him to be. If money was involved, it might be worth it.

"On one condition," I said while they all leaned forward intently, waiting for what that condition was.

"I get my own cabin and I get to go up one week early."

"Yes!" Queen celebrated while King leaned over and they high-fived me. "I knew it, I knew it," she replied, dancing in her chair. I laughed, which didn't happen very often until she asked me something she knew I would never say fucking yes to.

"Soooo, what about Cleo?"

With that, I hopped my ass up, took my coat and headed to the front door. Not one but two women had tried me today, and on a day I couldn't care less about.

"Knight!" Queen called out as she stood at the door. "Call me!"

At this point, fuck Queen, too.

4

NOEL LANCASTER

It was a week before Christmas, and I decided to head up to Mason with the kids. Neil and his girlfriend, Erin, who he'd been dating for a few months, would be up in a few days or so. And while I wasn't that excited to be in Mason without Desmond, it was a reminder that life goes on as I drove up and sang songs with Paige and PJ before they fell off to sleep. Once they did, I silently cried but reminded myself that I had more to offer than empty promises.

As we approached the last leg on I-10 to Mason, I looked in my rearview mirror and saw PJ with a cookie partially squished in his hand, drooling, while Paige clutched on tightly to her doll, causing me to smile. Cookie, our Labrador, stared back there, too, ensuring they were safe while keeping me up with occasional sniffs and licks on the jaw.

"Hello, Cookie, girl. How you are feeling over there?" I asked her as she leaned over, resting her chin on my lap as I drove.

"I know, honey," I said, rubbing the top of her head. "Tired of being in here, but we are almost there."

Mason was north of Jonestown, a small town up in the forestry part of state. Hunting and hiking were pretty popular if you weren't into the crowds that flocked about at the eateries, shops and local lounges. Mason was small, but lively, full of festivities for kids, families and couples.

It was a place where everything felt just right, and no one was in a rush to do anything but have a good time. And during Christmas, it morphed into a huge Wonderland of sorts with shoppers and Christmas carols being heard on every street.

The town literally lit up with holiday cheer as it transformed into a world full of glee of its own. People actually stopped and smiled, greeting and offering you compliments before they went on about their day. The hustle and bustle of Jonestown was easily a distant memory as Mason sucked you right on in and reminded you that there was love in the world from people all around. You just had to catch it and become one with it.

In fact, I obsessed with Mason, probably more than I cared to admit since Mason was where the first time *it* happened. It being Desmond and I finally making love three years ago. We were both just shy of twenty-one.

"Don't go," I whispered after he'd helped me into bed. We'd been out and about all day hiking, only stopping a time or two to eat and take in the scenery. The sun had set, and it was beyond beautiful. So beautiful, neither of us wanted to leave, but we had to or I'd be in a lot of trouble.

My parents already hated I'd rather be doing this than helping my mother and Nyla decorate the tree and prepare for Christmas dinner. I could cook, though. I had to learn since my mother wouldn't have it any other way, but there were times I could get out of it and Mason was one of them.

"Your leg?" he asked with concern since I'd scraped my shin on a rock. I refused to tell anyone out of fear of my parents not allowing me to hike again. They trusted Desmond, but just barely.

"Yes, can you pull the wrap off again so I can take a look? I think it's bleeding. We may need to add more gauze," I whispered, since the walls weren't as thick as I wished they could be. Trust me. I could hear Payne giving Nyla the business the night before, wondering how she could even walk, let alone stand to cook dinner.

"Sure," he said, sighing as he quietly reached inside my duffle bag to grab some peroxide and a few gauzes. "You're going to have to pull your tights off, Nollie," he instructed me as I sat up and winced.

"You can do it," I groaned as I fought hard not to scream. I was so going to get it if I did. Knowing my mother, the drama queen, a trip to the ER was in my future and I refused to spend my time here in some hospital. So, Desmond needed to move, and quickly.

"Which is why it happened. I pushed you to do it, to prove you could hike that high," he said with regret. I did, but my leg was proof I shouldn't' have when I looked down and slipped.

"It's fine, Dezzy. Trust me," I whimpered, as he tried to pull the leg of my tights up my calf with no success. "Just help me take these off," I fussed lowly, agitated.

"Y—you sure?" he stammered, then swallowed slow and hard. I already knew why, but it was that or me trying to do it myself, which I did before we arrived. Desmond turned his back the entire time to make sure no one was looking while I attended to my wound on the hiking trail. Clearly, I needed help. Not privacy.

"Please, Dezzy," I begged of him as I flopped back on the bed in pain.

"Okay," he gave in and motioned for me to raise up my hips. When I did, his fingers slid in the waistband of my tights and I shuddered. "It hurts?"

"No," I said quickly, yet my breathing was picking up. "Keep going."

His body was close, so close to mine with our orbs boring into each other. His breathing now matched mine. It was insane.

"What do you want me to do?" he asked, although I was sure that loaded question was asked for a different reason.

"To...keep going," I said as his lips grazed mine. Oh, fuck.

"Lift up easy, Nollie. I don't want to hurt you." I did, and with each tug, a peck on my lips followed as he slipped my tights over my ass. When he slipped his tongue in my mouth, I felt my heart beating in between my legs.

"Shit," he said, biting and pulling on my lip. "We are almost there," he said softly. I could hear an intensity in his voice coupled with the look in his eyes as my thighs appeared. "Shit, Nollie." A gentle rub of my thighs had me quivering before my panties followed. He leaned back and stared in awe as if he was seeing me for the first time.

"Wow," was what I heard next as our eyes connected. His hand traveled down to release my tights from my ankles. I couldn't believe this was happening. This was fucking happening.

He took his time kissing the back of my calf and then down my thigh before his face was nestled in between my legs. His eyes asked a question that had me screaming one thousand times yes as I panted in anticipation when he sniffed my pussy.

"Fuck, Nollie. Your pussy...it's...it's..."

He couldn't speak but he didn't have to when he parted my lower lips and eased his tongue inside, lapping up my love. Before I could even scream, he stuck his fingers in my mouth while he gave me the most earth-shattering orgasm as my legs splayed to each side. He then whispered, "Nollie, I want to make love to you."

And with an eager, willing nod because I'd lost my capacity to speak, I gave myself to my best friend and he took me and my entire existence with him.

Then over the next few days there, he started to move and act weird, getting missing to find things to do, which was strange since they all knew he came to be with me.

The morning on our way back, he told me he couldn't sleep. Said he feared crossing that boundary would change things until the plan he had in motion came into fruition. I thought he had to be kidding because the sex was fucking amazing, but sadly, he was right. We could barely be alone and not want each other, it was like a pressure pipe threatening to blow and I guess it did now in the form of a girlfriend. Fucking Desmond had no plan unless it was to fuck me over which he'd definitely done.

Once we pulled up to the cabin, I realized I was crying. Cookie refused to move, watching me quickly wipe the tears with the back of my hand. Soon, the kids began to squirm once they no longer felt the motion of the road. I quickly dabbed out of fear I'd upset them. No way was I about to let them see their Auntie Nollie crying.

"Hi, babies," I cooed and semi-recovered. I smiled as I looked in the rearview mirror to check out my eyes. They weren't puffy, but evidence of sadness still rested in the rims of my eyelids as I dabbed them once more. "Had a good nap?"

"Yup, and now it's time to go play," PJ said as he stretched and yawned before he greeted me with a smile.

"Yes, you can go play, but first, we need to get our things in the cabin and then you need to wash your faces. Once you do that, we can head on over to the Bookers to get some food." Paige celebrated while PJ groaned. He was such a boy. Cookie barked excitedly, waiting for me to let her out. It was showtime. I couldn't sit around here and pout with these two cuties reminding me we were in Mason.

"Welp, if you don't help me, PJ, then no trip to the Bookers. We just eat the rest of Grammy's sandwiches," I replied, fake pouting. "Oh, and applesauce."

"Fine," he grumbled as they both got out with Cookie in tow. In no time, their little smiles and chatter made my heart felt somewhat whole again. I may not have a best friend or even a boyfriend, but I did have these two little stinkers and Cookie, who loved me unconditionally. I just needed to get over it, and fast, to make the best of it.

Fuck Desmond. It was time for me to create new memories in Mason without him.

5

KNIGHT COMMODORE

"Knight, don't you think it's time we talked?" Rayelle asked, slipping onto the balcony while I sat there in peace, smoking my nightly blunt.

"About?" I replied, releasing the smoke through my nose as I watched the sunset. Today was a great day to do that as I grabbed my glass of bourbon. I was privately celebrating the deal we'd just closed on after we'd bailed out a state hospital that served people who looked like me. Healthcare was already shitty, so I wasn't surprised when I sat on the board and learned they were in dire straits financially. Being on the board is what Rayelle called a good look, and in true Rayelle fashion, CE was on the news in less than an hour with Channel 7 reporting our latest acquisition.

Once again, she'd somehow found a way to get back in my graces for simply doing her job, but she really did do it so well. Things had been touch and go since Thanksgiving dinner. Especially since each time she asked me about Mason, I changed the subject.

"Well, first, congratulations are due, Knight," she said, appearing to be genuine, I suppose. I used to suck at that, but I learned to study motherfuckers or get fucked over. Ray fucked me over in many ways when we were younger, making me feel shit, giving me hope in entertaining the idea of love. Too bad we were both too fucked up to believe we both could have that shit everyone else had. Her mother was just as fucked up as mine. She just hid hers well using her daughter as bartering tool for money when her pussy was too old to pay the bills.

She pretended she was doing what she had to do, but I'd fucking kill Cleo if she was tricking Queen off. It sort of made me feel sorry for Rayelle, but instead of her owning her fucked up ways like me, she tried to hide them, pretending she did love power the same way I did. I wasn't that little boy anymore getting fucked over by my mother and the system. I was grown fucking man and Rayelle knew it too, yet she still tried to play mind games being all nice.

Besides, in order to stay on top and remain powerful, I literally had to stay on top, if you know what I mean, starting with Rayelle who had exquisite pussy. Exquiste but a fucked up heart with her sneaky ass flaunting what I knew was some good pussy under them clothes in my face.

"Thanks, Ray. Appreciate that," I replied, hitting my blunt

once more as my eyes studied her body that stood between me and the sunset.

"Always. Anything for you," she lied with ease, but fuck it. I was going to make this last-minute visit work for me. She knew what she was doing as I studied her greatest asset called hips until my eyes traveled up and rested on her generous portion of breasts. Breasts I've had the pleasure of fucking before I released all over her mouth, chin and neck. Ray was a nasty bitch. I mean nasty. Folks wouldn't believe it if I told them, but at thirteen, it was her who turned my ass out. "But we do need...to talk," she spoke sultrily as I put my blunt down and gave her my full attention.

"I'm listening."

"Are you sure?" she probed as one hand traveled up my neck, followed by the gentle kneading of my flesh, causing me to grunt.

"Damn, Knight. You're tight, very tight," she whispered as she worked my neck slowly as I closed my eyes. "Wow," she said, before she took those same fingers and dragged them across my scalp, causing me to hiss. "How does that feel?"

I grunted as my reply, to which she used to keep on going. She worked my neck really good as she kneaded my flesh, creating small circles to relieve the tension. Tension I didn't even know I had when she leaned down and rested her lips against my ear.

"See, you needed that," I heard her say, her lips grazing

my ear. "Let me work that out for you, Knight...like only I can," she propositioned like a high-class, well-paid whore.

She then pushed her legs against mine before she inched closer and closer until those fat-ass breasts rested just shy of my lips. Lips she wanted on hers, I could tell, that formed an "O" shape.

"I miss you so much, Knight," she whispered, then shuddered when I slapped her ass. "Shit, baby. Yes," she repeated over and over as I slid my hands up her thighs, planting them underneath her ass. I was hungry for dinner before she had arrived, but I was even hungrier for this pussy. My cook, Genie, knew not to disturb, but even if she did, she was used to me fucking Ray all over my house, the balcony included.

"I'm so sorry about the other night. I just—"

"Shut the fuck up and take all this off," I commanded, disinterested in talking. It didn't matter what she said as long as this pussy was about to talk. Once she was totally nude as if we weren't outside, I took in her buttermilk body with pussy so slick and smooth. Keeping it real, I actually liked a little hair on my pussy, a landing strip, but I guess her other nigga, Stephen, that was hitting it couldn't handle a few whiskers in his mouth. I hope you caught that too. Stephen was my that same person we both lived with together in the group home and the same one I employed. I couldn't blame him though. I learned she turned him out too until I woke the fuck up. His soft ass reminded me why I never slid in her raw considering he was married, and she was his side bitch.

"Top drawer," I whispered forcefully. That was where I kept my supply of condoms as she groaned. "Or you can get dressed and leave."

"No, no. Just relax," she countered before she did as I instructed her to do. She'd better hurry up before I change my mind, and she did, rushing back to me naked with heels on.

Once she got me right and I inspected the condom while she smirked. Once it appeared to fully intact, I took her by both hips and whispered, "Sit on this motherfucker."

Besides her letting me rattle the back of her throat with my dick, foreplay was a thing of the past. It was straight gunplay in the pussy, no chaser.

"Don't you fucking move," I grunted, relishing in the tight warmth of her walls. I swear Stephen must have not been putting in that work because Ray stayed tight for me. I guess you're wondering why I'm still fucking her and she's still fucking him, huh? Easy, I don't give a fuck. He was in love with her. Not me.

"Knight, please," she cried out, wanting to take it for a ride, but she did too much howling and screaming like I was committing a fucking murder. I chuckled, understanding why since I did bring that work that was hard like bricks sold on the street. Mine, however, was called dick. This dick she just sat on and adjusted too like a big girl.

"Please, what?" I replied, slapping her ass two times as she yelped.

"Please, may I fuck you?"

"You might as well," I said more to myself as I slowly began to fuck her from underneath. She figured this would change my mind about Mason, but it only proved why she could never be more than this. My family was all kinds of fucked up but we survived. We made it work and if Queen said no, it was a hell no. Simple. "Stop fucking play, Ray," I huffed, popping that buttery ass thigh that turned red. "Don't come over here giving me some lazy pussy. I worked hard today enough already, right?"

"Yes, Knight, baby." She knew I didn't care for that baby shit, but she did exactly what I said, twerking like I'd a private show in a strip club except we were out in the open on my balcony.

As soon as I was about to release, Rayelle hopped down and took me in her mouth, suctioning all of my kids out. I told you she was a nasty bitch as I held her nose, daring her not to swallow every drop. Once I was done, I pushed her mouth off of me and she sat up and smiled evilly. Crazy ass.

She was pleased with her performance while I was honestly disgusted. She had plenty of money she'd made from working at CE. Hell, any man in Jonestown would want her, yet she chose to be sidelined by not one but two men.

And before she could open her mouth to set up her proposal about Mason, I stood up and walked inside my bedroom. I went straight to the bathroom to shower with the door locked and all, shutting that shit down.

"Thanks, Ray. Stellar performance, baby girl. See you tomorrow at work," I called out to her as I disrobed. Once I did, I stepped in the shower where nothing but hot water clawed at my angry soul. I hated Cleo ass for making me despise love and Rayelle for proving all women were like Cleo—incapable of keeping shit real and dealing with the cards life had dealt you responsibly.

6

NOEL LANCASTER

"NOEL," MRS. BOOKER GREETED ME AS I WALKED IN. SHE THEN clapped her hands with excitement when the kids and Cookie appeared. Thank God they were a pet-friendly store. They always were and were staples in the town of Mason, along with a few others business owners that made it seem like we were always welcomed. Even Cookie, who had waited for Mrs. Booker to gently rub the top of her head. "Now, you two, don't be shy. Where's my hug?" The kids crashed into her body where she greeted them with kisses on the cheek as she rubbed their shoulders.

"They've gotten so big, Noel."

"Tell me about it," I groaned when I realized how much money I was about to blow in here. Neil would be up in a few days, so it was my job to make sure we all didn't starve until then.

"Noel," Mr. Booker called out to me, coming from the back. "I knew one of you Lancasters would ease in here soon. A bit early, though."

"The weather. We wanted to get up here before it started coming down. You know my mother hates when any of us drive in the snow."

"Ah, yes," he said. "It has started early. Came in to get supplies?" he asked me as I smiled.

"Uh, I wouldn't know what all we have or need back at the cabin. Sort of Neil's or my dad's department. I came with my hunter's gun, hiking boots and a stomach waiting to eat all kinds of crap," I told him honestly with a shrug.

I could eat for three people and not gain a pound while Nyla swore looking at a piece of cheesecake added inches to her waist. I naturally had a good metabolism but staying active outdoors when I wasn't working at the pet store caused me to have a hearty appetite, though my size four wouldn't show it.

"Well, we have plenty. Heard the snow will be coming down hard this week, so check out some lamp oils, wood logs, candles, canned good items like tuna, bread, some sweets—"

"Sweets, Auntie Nollie!" the kids cried out in unison as he chuckled. I guess they ignored the whole snow coming down hard part, but I was used to snow. I guess they were, too, running past me to follow him down the sweets aisle.

"Since he has them, let me show you what I just whipped

up last night," she smiled, ducking down with a container of my favorite—peanut brittle.

"Mrs. Booker! My favorite."

"I know. I haven't weighed and priced them yet, but here," she whispered, slipping me two bags. "I will just add a few bucks to the final balance," she told me, knowing she'd make that back and more from me alone by the time I left Mason.

Once she did, I took a stroll through the store. I grabbed a few things to snack on like chips, soup, and hot cereal like oatmeal. I even grabbed me a few candles and body soaks for my evening baths. I may be a tomboy, but I still enjoyed pampering myself when I could. Especially since working at the pet store was practically a 24/7 day gig for me. That left little time to schedule a freaking spa day.

By the time the kids were done and our items were rung up, I gasped when I realized I didn't have my purse. "Oh, no."

"What happened, Auntie Nollie?" Paige asked sweetly, sucking on a lollipop I'm more than sure Mr. Booker had slipped in her hand.

"I sort of left my purse," I told her with a tight smile, hating we would have to come back. PJ's forehead crinkled like *why did that matter* as he smacked on a cookie he was eating. Another cookie, right? We should have named him that instead of the dog.

His face looked how I felt, but it was what it was. I figured if we had to go back, I could at least check out if we had any supplies back at the cabin to hold us over if there weren't many supplies there.

"Oh no, dear," Mrs. Booker said, looking at the five to six bags of crap we had piled up ready to go. "Uh..."

"I think I can handle this...*Auntie Nollie*," a gentleman offered, grinning as he gazed down at the kids with amusement. Paige was batting her honey-colored eyes while PJ was wagging his tongue with chocolate chip crumbs around his mouth. A few missing teeth made him appear to be harmless, but I wanted to warn this guy that they could be little savages.

"Are—are you sure?" I barely got out, wondering how and when heaven dropped all of this dark chocolate colored goodness on earth as he smiled. When he did, I panicked. "Wait! Please don't. I can just come back." But tell that to these kids when they yelled thank you and snatched their bags off the counter while Cookie celebrated with them as she ran around in circles.

"It's fine. I promise. They're happy, you're happy. I mean, you are happy, right?" he asked. When he did, it as if he were studying me like maybe I had something on my face.

I wiped it a few times, which caused him to laugh I guess. I just wasn't sure if it were appropriate to ask him or Mrs. Booker why he was looking at me like that. Then asking me if I'm happy made me wonder if he was flirting but why would he? And with me? Oh fuck no. Especially since I was just dumped by the only man to even say he loved me. Clearly no one else was checking for me if I only had one man to referenced in the department of heartbreak. I was screwed, so screwed as I tried to speak but nothing would come out.

"Noel, honey. Are you okay?" Mrs. Booker asked, then nervously looked his way when he handed her his credit card.

"Yes...yes, I am," I lied, sniffling as I was on the verge of crying all over again. I hated Desmond. I swear I fucking did. "Just allergies. Freaking allergies," I lied as she snapped me out of my fog.

"Then that's all that matters, right?" he assured me, standing so close to me as he swiped his credit card. When I thought I'd recovered from being goofy, weird or whatever it was I'm sure he'd concluded about me, he leaned over and whispered, "You should take something for those allergies. You're too pretty to be...sniffling from allergies." I lost it, his woody scent cologne tickling my nose. Gosh, I was in love... Wait. I wasn't but just that quickly, he'd brainfucked me.

"Good idea," Mrs. Booker chimed in. "I can add some allergy meds. Just a second, " she said, taking off and leaving us alone. I mean, *alone* alone while she went to the back. I tried looking at everything and anything but him, but there he was, just standing right there, and sizing me up as I heard a hum here or there. I even thought a hiss slipped through his lips but for what? I looked like a freaking boy with baby boobs.

I was not only embarrassed but about to have a panic

attack while he stood there confidently, looking like a walking billboard of money from his Louis Vuitton tennis shoes and wallet, which didn't go unnoticed, with dark brown jeans that hung off his hip, revealing bowed legs. His tan sweater housed a mass of well-defined abs and chest I couldn't even imagine how they would feel, yet almost did as he eased up on me.

"Whoever he is is a fucking asshole," he whispered in my ear. "You're too pretty to be crying. I'm sorry for saying that shit, but it's true, *Auntie Nollie*," he added with a smile that created a pool of moisture in between my thighs.

The Auntie Nollie caused me to snicker as I blinked both of my eyes, fighting hard not to have a total meltdown and snot all over the place in front of him. He made it easy though, inviting even as he looked at me with perhaps empathy. His words alone told me he didn't have time for someone feeling sorry for themselves.

"It's Noel," I corrected him in between sniffles, still laughing. I don't know why but hearing him call me that was hilarious. Either that or I just needed a laugh. It didn't matter though because I was feeling better.

"I actually like Auntie Nollie but remember what I said. Fuck him," he told me as Mrs. Booker made her way back over to the register with some Claritin. He knew I didn't need it, but I was thankful he didn't blow my cover.

"I think that's all, Mister..."

"Knight. Just Knight," he told her, then shot a wink my

way as I studied him even more now that I could see a bit clearer as I dabbed my eyes.

He had bushy eyebrows that rested over lazy, warm, cedar brown eyes with thick lips and a full beard. He was tall, too. Very tall. And when he bidded me a goodbye with no offer of me repaying him back, I blinked instead. I fucking blinked. Gosh, I'm such an idiot.

As I stood there waiting for my brain to process this whatever this was was over, he took charge with no guidance from me as I watched him settle the kids and Cookie down as he grabbed my bags.

"Wait, I need to pay you back," I said quickly as I came to, patting my pockets to grab my cell phone. I needed his address or at least his number so I could transfer the money.

"Auntie Nollie, are you okay?" my nephew PJ asked me, while this Knight guy gave me a look as if I'd insulted him. Too bad since I wasn't accepting charity. Besides, he was just being a nice guy, and trust me, nice people always came in last.

That's me. I'm nice people.

"Put it away, Noel," he demanded lowly but firmly, no smile in sight. Damn, he said that like we were cool, friends even when we'd just met all of ten minutes ago as I rolled my eyes "Now, which car, and if you ever try to repay someone for doing what any decent human being should do, then don't," he said, shutting me down.

This man, with mere words, had shut me up while Paige

looked on, smiling and swaying like she was watching a movie. Cookie was eating the last of PJ's cookie while Knight called my name again in a demanding tone.

"Noel...show me the way," he told me, his patience clearly running short with me as I opened my mouth. "Say less," he warned me, his jaw twitching.

"Fine. Right this way...assshole," I grumbled, praying he didn't hear me. I suppose he didn't or if he did, he chose to let it go. "Oh, and we walked," I told him, smiling. The kids needed air and I needed to clear my head. See how screwed up I was after picking up six bags of crap. Insane for sure.

"Guess we are together a little bit longer," he said, motioning with his head for us to follow up. And let me tell you, that sight from behind did not disappoint. I was going to need a bath and release. I had no clue who this Knight was, but I was staying the fuck away from him right after I found out how to pay him back.

7

KNIGHT COMMODORE

"You look happy today, Knight. Very happy," my therapist Miss Reynolds said, before taking a sip of her coffee, which made me feel warm. I loved seeing her lips the same color as that coffee pressed up against the outside of the mug. And slow, too. In fact, Miss Reynolds did everything slow, never in rush. Especially during therapy.

"I guess," was all I replied, fighting hard to suppress that stupid grin I wore in her presence without even knowing it. King would catch it all the time, teasing me while Queen would roll her eyes. "I'm alright," I added with a nod as I lifted my eyes before lowering them again.

"You are more than alright, Knight. It's been four years since we started, and you have made wonderful progress. More than you care to admit. I'd say that's a reason to be happy, no?"

"If you mean not knocking a motherfu—I mean a dude out for

looking at Queen, then yes. I'm learning. Besides, it's all in the presentation...the scowl. Queen's beautiful, so I get it...like you," I added, shooting her a look as she laughed.

"Actually, it's called better coping skills. However, if a mean face works, then so be it. You are using your words and a better selection at that. I've watched you, so great work," she said, almost whispering as she leaned in closer to me. "How are things at home with your mother?"

"You mean Cleo?"

"Yes, Knight. Cleo."

By then, the state had returned us home with Cleo, and the only thing I loved about it was being with my brother and sister. Cleo could choke on her vomit while sucking a dick for all I cared. We'd been back with her for two years now. Since then, we'd only had a few incidents of her getting missing, but nothing the state knew about unless Miss Reynolds didn't count. She was cool as hell, though. Sneaky, but cool as she tricked me into talking when no one else could.

"Cleo is Cleo. Same sh—I mean, same person, just a different program," I replied, being honest. She was the same. She just replaced one poison for another. One that was legally prescribed and monitored, instead of a bottle.

"A different program is progress, Knight. Now she needs something else and you do, too."

"Yeah?" I replied with a lift of the brow. "Like what?"

That bitch needed to have terminated her parental rights long ago, but she hadn't. Her womb should have been labeled expired as a warning sign before my father slid in her. It probably wouldn't have mattered, though. Not if he were like most men when they were young who were obsessed with fat asses and pretty smiles because Cleo was beautiful. Still, he loved her, and she loved him. Another reason why I wasn't fucking with love. Look where it had gotten them.

"Forgiveness, Knight. Imagine all the possibilities that could come with that," she said, her golden streaks in her hair giving her cinnamon complexion more of a glow. I knew I knew nothing about love, but Miss Reynolds did make me feel funny in my stomach all the time. I like that shit. I liked that shit a lot.

"Knight? Um, Knight?" I heard her say, unsure of how long I had zoned out when I snapped my head in her direction. "I was only about to ask you to unlock the door," Noel said with a look of concern in her eyes.

And then it hit me why I was so taken by her. She reminded me of Miss Reynolds from the warm brown cinnamon complexion and golden brown locs of hair. Her smile, although it looked painful when she did smile the few times she did, was infectious. It made me want to smile, giving me that funny feeling in my stomach like I had many years ago.

"Ye—yeah. I got it. Sorry about that," I stammered before clearing my throat.

"It's fine," she said, looking down and chewing her lip while the kids were laughing and talking amongst themselves in the back. It's like every time I glanced her way, she avoided making eye contact with me. "I guess," she mumbled, shifting in her seat as she looked out the window.

"Yeah okay," I told her, shaking my head. This girl was a trip. One second she was hot, the next cold. Beautiful, but definitely making me wonder if old boy was right for cutting her ass off. "And don't touch those bags. either," I instructed her once I unlocked the door as she sucked her teeth.

"Yayyy," they yelled, jetting out with their dog right behind them as they ran to the front of the cabin.

"You know you don't have to do this. I already owe you money," she told me before I stepped out of my truck.

"And I don't need to be told what I don't need to do," I replied, taking her in when she tugged on the door for it to open when I locked it again.

"Are you serious right now?" she asked me with bucked eyes.

"I don't know. Maybe I am. Maybe I'm not," I teased her, loving how she twisted her lips when she was frustrated. She'd been doing that the entire ride each time she caught me glancing at her. I was surprised I hadn't ran into anything on the way back the way she had my fucking head spinning. Especially when Miss Reynolds crossed my mind, tugging on my heart even in my memories.

I'd done the work to be a productive citizen and not a habitual juvie offender. So, I know Miss Reynolds would be proud of me now. Well, except the fact that I still wasn't messing with Cleo.

"So are we going to just sit in here or let my niece and nephew freeze?" she probed through slitted eyes. Noel was a trip. Those kids could give two fucks about playing outside, not giving us a care in the world and she knew it too. Still, I entertained her feisty ass.

"They are hardly freezing, but I will, under one condition."

"Condition? Oh, no," she said, pulling forcefully on the door handle. "Let me get you your money right now. I'm not that kind of girl, *Knight*."

"You're right. You're not that kind of girl, *Noel*," I said, wondering why a girl like her was even single. Sure, she was moody, but she was fine as fuck. A little thin for my taste, but she didn't let those jeans make it at all and her ass. Wow, Noel's ass was ripe for the picking. I'd have her hemmed up on the hood of this truck and eat her up for dinner once the kids were put down for bed.

And I could tell she had a good heart, looking out the window at her niece and nephew who she clearly loved the same way I loved Mallory and MJ.

You're fucking up, Knight boy. Chill.

"Thank you. I appreciate you saying that," she said, conceding just a little as she crossed her arms. I actually liked the little banter we had going, but I was a fucked up individual. Sure, I had money and gave it away at the drop of a dime to damn near anyone in need, but she was already crying over a dude. No need in me adding to the bullshit when all I had to offer was my wallet and dick.

"Let me get you and your things inside," I told her, deciding to put some space in between us before I went into unchartered territory. Besides, I didn't come up here to link up with a woman. I came to clear my head and then check into snatching up a few cabins for CE if the numbers added up.

Once I stepped out, I felt the wind blowing as the sun began to set. Snow was definitely coming, which meant for a few days, I'd be inside. Good thing I'd already had enough supplies and a generator inside my cabin should the power go out. That was a must because I wasn't about to thug it out in no cold-ass cabin alone with no internet.

I was still excited about the hospital, eager to go inside and come up with a few things I wanted to run by Queen and King. That was much safer for me than trying my luck with Noel. I didn't even know what that would look like and really wasn't interested the more I thought about it as I grabbed the bags and locked up the truck to take them inside.

"Mr. Knight, are you coming back?" her niece, Paige, asked sneakily when Noel shot her a look. Her cinnamon complexion was now flushed as Paige snickered. Yeah, she was definitely like my niece, Mallory.

"I'm sure I'll see you all around before I head on back home in a week or so. Make sure you listen to your Auntie Nollie, too. She seems tired. I think she's had enough of me anyway," I slid in, smiling just to mess with her when she squinted her eyes my way. "You know how cranky babies act when they are tired."

"Yep, like PJ. Mommy be saying, 'boy, go sit down before I knock you down with your cranky self. You tired. Just tired'. Right, Auntie Nollie?" she giggled, impersonating her mother.

"Oh, God. Get inside. All three of you," she ordered them, playfully swatting them as they rushed past her. "And you, wait right there," she told as she marched off.

As I waited, I decided to take a look around the cabin. It was smaller than mine, much smaller, but inviting. It felt and looked lived in with a tiny fireplace that sat bare with no logs. I was already overstepping my boundaries as I made a mental note to bring some by before nightfall.

The appliances needed upgrading but it was clean. Very clean. The wood cabinets were solid that needed a little varnish. My mind began to spin as I took in the condition of the floors. They were wooden, and creaked a little, but I liked the sound of it as I paced from one end of the living room to the next.

I must have waited about ten minutes when I realized she'd been gone a while, then I heard her grunt and grumble to herself. I even heard her tossing things around before she marched back out to the living room close to tears.

"Uh-oh. She's crying again after Desmond decided to

dump her," Paige whispered very loudly from the room they were in.

"That's not her boyfriend, silly girl. He's *just* her friend," her nephew, PJ, shot back in defense. I liked that shit. I hope this Desmond guy got his ass whooped, too.

"Kissing friends? Friends kiss? Ugh, I don't want no boys kissing on me."

"Good because I don't know any boys that would want to," he shot back when we heard a pop sound followed by a scream. Damn, these two little ones were savages.

"Ugh, I can't take it anymore," she belted, then slid down the wall until her ass was now rested on the floor. "I can't," she said, closing her eyes as tears rolled down her cheeks. "I just can't."

"Yes, you can," I told her, walking over and kneeling down. "Everyone needs a little help sometimes, Noel. Hell, even me."

Did I really say that? I was starting to scare my-damn-self, wondering what was in the air in Mason because I hadn't smoked shit. I didn't even have any blunts, choosing not to travel with anything that could lead to those boys fucking with me.

I guess something was in the air when an hour later, we were in the dining room eating and, surprisingly, having a ball. We were good and full and now I was in the kitchen helping her clean up. Imagine that. What the fuck?

"You know you didn't have to do any of this," she said as

we stood next to each other, washing dishes which was another "whoa" moment for me. Especially when the only woman I'd ever done that with was Queen. I'm telling you, it was getting weirder and weirder by the second. And when she smiled, the way she crinkled her nose made me literally want to lean over and kiss it. Me, Knight Commodore, kissing women on the nose?

Oh, hell no!

"I know you think I'm some ditzy, dysfunctional girl, but really, I'm not," she offered, her smile dissipating when she did. "I still can't believe I left my purse back home and I'm practically on empty in my tank. What was I even thinking?" she asked herself, handing me a glass since I took the lead on rinsing.

"I don't know, but what I do know is you can't allow a motherfucker to control this," I told her, tapping the side of my head. I wanted to say heart, too, but her niece and nephew already had her snotting earlier. I wasn't too fond of this Desmond guy, but I did know that whoever he was, he had a stronghold on her. She could pretend all she wanted to, but that fuck boy had her heart.

"Besides, I'm sure there's a gang of dudes lined up to stretch across Mason to get at you," I told her, lightly bumping her shoulders. "Stop playing now. You know I'm right, girl."

"Please," she chuckled, shaking her head. "Have you seen this chest and limited edition of hips and ass?"

Shit, she should have already known I'd seen all of that and while she didn't think it was much, I was fucking with her in the looks department. That was the one problem I had with women. They assumed shit about what a man wanted and liked, thinking like a woman when men were thinking like men. We liked them all and even if we didn't, some motherfucker would like Noel just the way she was...like me.

"I'm trying to now. Step back and let Knight see what you're working with, girl," I teased as I leaned back before she splashed a few suds my way.

"Oh, I know you didn't," I chortled, wiping my eyes before I lifted the suds and splashed them back her way. She squealed, causing the kids and their dog to come rushing in the kitchen, only for them to egg us on.

"Ugh, I'm all wet," she finally said once she realized her shirt was soaked. I couldn't help but notice it as her nipples rose to the occasion from the cool air. "Knight!" she playfully fussed. "I so owe you. I'm telling you I do," she belted, tossing her head back when her nose crinkled up again, and guess what I did then.

I kissed her nose. I fucking kissed it.

8

NOEL LANCASTER

After we'd cleaned up the kitchen and I slipped into something dry, I peeked down the hall to make sure the past few hours weren't a figment of my imagination.

I blinked a few times until I thought he had looked down the hallway before I stuck my head back in the bedroom.

"Shoot, shoot, shoot," I fussed lowly as I stood still as if he could see me through the walls. Cookie blew my cover, barking as she ran down the hall and stood in front of the door. "Go, go away," I whispered forcefully when she hopped up and almost knocked me down. "Cookie!" I yelped, laughing as she licked my face.

Everyone wanted to play today, but the more I thought about it, I'd been laughing since Knight had walked into my life down at the Bookers' store.

"It's time for bed, Cookie," I told her, sitting up as I

rubbed her neck. "We have a long day tomorrow. We have a tree to put up, so get some rest," I told her as her eyelids began to close. "Goodnight, girl," I whispered before she took off. I sauntered back into the living room where he was still sitting with a smile on his face.

"You're smiling," I told him, hoping he'd forgotten I was peeking, but I could tell he hadn't.

"And you are, too. You suck at hiding."

"Tell me something else I don't know."

"Well...you're beautiful Shit, beyond beautiful. I feel simple as fuck since I can't even come up with a word to describe you to be honest," he said, catching me off guard.

"Wow," was all I said before I looked at him suspiciously, tucking my legs underneath me. "You're not playing with me now, are you? Feeling sorry for me?"

"I wish I was, but now. I'm for real. More than you know, Noel. Before I could respond, he asked, "Kids down?"

It wasn't what he said, but *how* he said it that made me nod, losing my voice.

"Noel? Words work better for me. I'm a man of few words to be honest, but right about now, I need them shits and bad," he whispered, motioning for me to sit closer to him. "My head cloudy," he said although I think he was speaking more to himself than me.

"Okay," I sang and scooted slowly closer to him. "And to answer your question. Yes, they are down. Bath, nighttime prayer and tucked all in."

Damn, why did I say tucked all in? The idea alone of being tucked under his massive, yet toned arm seemed foreign, but something I sure wouldn't mind. Desmond was a man, but Knight was *all man*. He was *that man*. I could tell that the second he stepped in front of me at the store and then bullied his way into our cabin.

"It's late," I told him, fidgeting as I watched him rubbed his fingers up and down his thigh. Shit, why did he do that?

"It is," he said as he stood up and sighed I guess hearing my thoughts. This was starting to become...hard. Dang, I didn't mean hard but it was hard not looking at the damage he was blessed with as he slid his hands in his jean pockets, which made the blessing before me just the obvious.

I was sure I must have had an eye blinking condition when he bellowed loudly before he caught himself, looking down the hallway where the kids were.

"Sorry," I said and chuckled, pinching my eyes together just one before I stretched them. I'm such a goof ball. This man just told me how beautiful I am and I fucking blink...again. Ugh.

"Don't be," he said with a shrug as I stood. "They're tired."

"That they are. I will have to pry them out of bed. Trust me." I couldn't even move once I stood, watching him dragging his hand down his mouth where a smile once appeared. It was him that was a beautiful, rocking a beautiful set of pristine white teeth that were accompanied by his soul snatching smile. Yes, I said it. It was indeed soul snatching since I almost needed him to help me move when he smiled again. "I'm think going to call you Smiley," I told him, I'm sure while blushing as he gazed down at me.

"Smiley?" He chuckled, but it was short lived as he became serious again, his stare now a piercing one as I squirmed.

"Well, you have been smiling since you've met me.. I'm just saying. The proof is standing in front me," I replied back this time sassily, wondering where this new boldness came from. Wait, it wasn't me. It was my girl between my legs chattering away. She wanted Knight in the worse way. She was going to get me into trouble.

Scratching the back of his neck, he laughed lowly as he watched my feet shift as I put weight on one leg after taking it off of the other. I needed to run and fast and he knew it, nodding his head as if we were speaking to each other telepathically.

"Lock up, Noel. And if you never believe a man every again in life, remember that you're beautiful. Inside and out, love. Make sure you remember that if we never get a chance to hang out and rap again," he told me as his smile faded.

"Leaving Mason?" I probed, close to begging him to stay.

"No, but you didn't come to Mason to hang out with a stranger."

"I don't know. Try me. Maybe I did," I tossed back, hoping he'd catch it. "Tomorrow night at eight. A Christmas tree decoration extravaganza," I said excitedly since our tree was being delivered tomorrow.

"You sure?" he asked, easing up closer to me where goosebumps greeted him as he looked down at me. And as predicted, he smiled.

"I'm uh, sure," I barely got out, wishing his mouth was all over me. Fuck, I was being a whore hearing Nyla's advice about a one-night stand. Me? Noel Lancaster and a one-night stand? No fucking way.

"You don't sound so sure, but let's see what happens," he said, leaning over and kissing me on the top of my head, my dread bun dangling to the side. I could have sworn I heard him inhale but he had pulled back too quickly for me to confirm. My center knew he did as she did a little two step inside of my panties, eager to write home to tell anyone that would listen that maybe, just maybe, I really had a reason to move on. "Tomorrow at eight?"

"Yes, tomorrow at eight." Oh God, I was so fucked. Mason really was doing a number on me and fast.

9

KNIGHT COMMODORE

IRONICALLY, AS BEAT AS I WAS, I COULD BARELY SLEEP A WINK. I sat up most of the night since I'd left Noel and the kids doing what I thought I would never do when it came to a woman. That was lowkey study her. Well, not her exactly, although I did look across the way to see if she was still up until all the lights in the cabin went off.

Sadly, the kids were right as I perused through years and years of posts, uploaded photos and videos where she and Desmond were beyond best friends. I knew love when I saw it even if I didn't believe in it for myself.

Her Facebook page captions were "bestie this" and "bestie that" while they both seemed to carry a love in their eyes for each other. Then there was a turning point close to about six months ago. She posted less and then when she did post something, it appeared to be a random thought but it was anything but random.

That fucker had broken her heart.

She tried to fight through it, I could tell, especially in pictures she'd taken with her sister Nyla, who was pretty dolled up and definitely a bit more feminine in a prissy kind of way. Studying her darker maple brown complexion was nice, but something about Noel's smooth, flawless, cinnamon hue made it hard for me not to reach out and touch her. I was surprised I'd only snuck in a kiss on top of her head.

Her dread locs smelled so fucking good, too. I groaned, then felt my own nature rise.

"Oh, hell no." I sat up and shook my head, wondering if I could manage to be so close yet so far for a week. Hell, it blew my mind when I found out her cabin was right next to mine too. Some would call it fate, but fate wasn't fucking with Knight Commodore. Money was, but fate was a different story. Especially when it came to women.

I swiped my cell screen when I tried to close it when the next picture of her appeared. She was...breathtaking. It was a memory she shared when she first started growing her locs. Locs that she liked to wear perched up in a nice bun on her head. A few dangled and drifted to the side of her face and off her shoulder. She was sexy as fuck, too, with thin-rimmed glasses. She hadn't worn any since our paths had crossed either, which meant she either wore contacts lenses or they were just a photo prop.

I even dare say she looked like a naughty schoolteacher, sporting an educated look with loose, boyfriend jeans and a white tank that showed her golden, cinnamon-brown skin.

I started to feel like an obsessed high school kid that would gladly knock Desmond on his ass. So, it was good thing he did ditch her and, hopefully, kept it at that when she got back to Jonestown. I hadn't shared I was from there and was more stoked to know I'd been to her family pet store a time or two for MJ and Mallory.

Mallory owned a teacup while MJ had a German Shepherd. He told me that boys didn't care for teacups because nothing was cute about a dog that yelped like an annoying girl. I think that's why I vibed so hard with Paige and PJ because those two reminded me of my Mallory and MJ. They nitpicked and fussed with each other all day but would back each other up in a lie and not bat an eye while telling it.

When I looked at the time, it was now past one o'clock in the morning. The wind had picked up and I noticed the snow was starting to pour down steadily.

"No Christmas tree extravaganza," I said to myself, closing my eyes as I rested my head on both hands. Soon, strong gusts of wind came, rattling the windows for a steady two to three minutes.

"Damn, I can't sleep," I complained. I decided to head downstairs to pour me a shot of bourbon. By the time I did, the lights flickered. Immediately, I thought of Noel and the kids. We'd had such a good time, I didn't even remember to make sure they were good on supplies after I saw their empty fireplace.

I was debating if I should get dressed and take a sprint over there, when I heard a banging on the door.

"What the hell?" I spat as I snatched the door open, fuming until I saw it was Noel. She was standing there in tears, shivering as the snow beat against her body.

I pulled her in quickly, then looked around and asked, "Really, Noel? Where are the kids, love? Please don't tell me you left the kids."

"I—I couldn't carry them both. The electricity is out, and we don't…" she said, her voice trailing off as she started to cry again.

"Stay right here and don't move," I told her, meaning it as I slipped on my boots and coat by the door and took off. Cookie was standing vigilantly as soon as I opened the door, seemingly glad to see me as she nuzzled her nose against my leg. A few whimpers could be heard as the howling wind picked up.

"It's okay, girl. I got you," I told her. "Watch my back," I said, heading down the hall to the kids' room. Even though my adrenaline was rushing, I had to laugh because Noel was right. They could sleep through anything. Paige had her legs thrown across PJ, who was snoring.

"Guess it's just me," I told Cookie as I lifted Paige first, who mumbled, "I didn't do it. It was PJ that ate the brittle."

She was a lowkey snitch. Her snitching ass had slipped in her sleep as she hugged my neck tightly.

"Yeah, yeah," was all I said before I grabbed her coat by the door. Tossing it over her, I sprinted to my cabin while Cookie barked from the door of the cabin the entire time. By the time I made it back for PJ, Cookie was right there and was ready to go. For the second time in less than twenty-four hours, this girl had put me to work and I was wet.

"I'm so, so sorry," she groaned once we had the kids tucked in where Cookie fell off to sleep on the side of their bed.

"For what, Noel? You're responsible for the snowstorm? Wait, no, can't be that. I got it," I said, snapping my fingers. "It's the electricity. You're not slick," I said to her, grinning. "You knocked the electricity out just so you can come over here...and be with me." And by the time she tried to deny it, there was no space between us as I barricaded her body with both hands pressed firmly against the door.

"I can't...I can't...breathe," she said, blinking her eyes. It was dark, pitch dark, but after my eyes adjusted to the darkness, I could see her so clearly, as if she were standing under the sun. When she blinked a few more times, I hollered. She'd been blinking those damn eyes all day. I was convinced she needed some damn glasses now.

"That would mean you need me to breathe for you, Noel. Let me do that. Let me breathe for you," I whispered in her ear, no fucking laughing coming from me right about now. I was mesmerized. I wanted me some Noel Lancaster and not just her pussy. I wanted her period.

It was crazy how in one day, I not only became someone I didn't even fucking know, but my body wasn't even my own. Not when she controlled the hairs on my skin that were now raised as she whispered, "Yes."

"Come on," I told her as I backed up, slipping my hand into hers. When she didn't move, I realized she didn't want me to take control. She *needed* me to. She didn't trust her own thoughts, her own body. "Noel, love...come," I said firmly. "Let me take care of you and them, love." I had to add them, or I'd have her little ass hemmed up against the wall, eating her pussy until morning time.

It was a good thing I was fully stocked. I had plenty of stuff—lamps, a generator, flashlights, you name it. Even a huge deep freezer out back to put the food in to keep it cold if need be. But I didn't need any of that shit right now. I just wanted this beauty in bed with me, and not to fuck. Not right now. I even looked down at my dick and begged his ass to behave. She wasn't *that girl* and thank God she wasn't.

One day then turned into a few days and for the first time, I looked around and felt like I had a family. Imagine that. Me, Knight Commodore, with a family that wasn't Queen and King. I smiled as I walked around and saw kid shoes, tablets and everything on the floor. It felt peaceful, so peaceful until I woke up and the lights were back on when I saw the lamp outside lit up and she did, too, as we laid curled up on the floor together. Then it that didn't bring us back to reality, a voice outside that was yelling her name did.

"What's next?" I asked her when he called her name out again and this time with an attitude. It was rough and disturbing. Her body stiffened unlike mine as I shot up with clenched fists. We were wrapped up in a blanket, chilling in front of the fireplace. That meant this visitor wasn't leaving peacefully. I didn't' give a fuck it we had just met. He didn't have to act like that when it came to her at all.

Shit, I was hoping it was old boy so I could tell him to move the fuck on. He couldn't' have her back. Not Noel. Hell no. She'd come into my life, and in a matter of days made me, Knight Commodore, enjoy the simple things in life. She was cool as cucumber, too, with her forgetful, goofy ass. We could vibe, talking about anything and everything while the kids and Cookie had their run of the cabin.

No matter how many times Noel told them to chill and go sit down, I shushed her. Shit like toys and electronic devices were replaceable, but what's not is your childhood. I was able to live through them, getting a kick out of them playing and fighting only to go back to playing again. I even found a couple of movies that were kid-friendly, one being the *Wizard of Oz.* It was the version with Michael Jackson and Diana Ross. Shit was old even when I was a kid, but one of Queen's favorites. Still is, even today.

Things had gotten so relaxed, we even spooned as she allowed me to fuck up her hair and play in it. Noel was cool as fuck, and if I could have it my way, having her in my life beyond Mason was a must. She didn't know it, but I hoped she understood it wasn't up for discussion. Fuck what Rayelle thought. This was the perfect time to eliminate her ass.

"Hold up," I told her as I released her and headed for the door. When I opened it, dude was close to banging on it again and he was mad. Good thing he was because I was madder.

"Aye, Noel over? If she is, tell her to get the kids, Cookie, and let's go."

"And who the hell are you?" I asked, chuckling since he looked like he wanted to beat my ass.

"Someone you do not want to fuck with," he tried to assure me, but I was with the shits today. I guess Noel knew it, too, when she slid underneath my arm, rubbing sleep out of her eyes.

"Neil, really?" she spat, rolling her eyes.

"Damn, Noel," he snickered. "You moved on fast. No more Dezzy?"

"Don't," she warned me, placing her hand on my chest. "That's my brother, the asshole."

"That's my brother, the asshole," he mocked her. "Just come on. And you," he said, staring at me like he wanted this smoke. "I don't play about her."

"Good, 'cause I don't play about her, either," I told him, leaning down and softly kissing her on the top of her head. I patted her ass too for shits and giggles, then whispered, "Thank you for hanging out with me. Let's do this again. Cool?"

"Ah, ye—yeah," she stammered when her brother grunted. Fuck him.

"You sure?"

"I'm sure, Knight. And thank you for everything. I mean it, too," she told me as she blushed and for the first time, she didn't blink. Not at all. Damn, she was doing something to me. Thank God for Mason. I was about to buy up all these damn cabins and more.

10

NOEL LANCASTER

ONCE THE KIDS WERE BACK TO SLEEP ONCE KNIGHT BROUGHT them over from our cabin, I sat up all curled on the sofa in front of the fireplace, fighting hard to wake up. While I didn't not trust Knight, I didn't know him well enough to actually fall asleep when we first got there. I was still beating myself up, and here he was once again, saving me from myself.

"Noel?" Knight called out to me from the kitchen with a mug in his hand. "Have some?" I shook my head no since I already had to tinkle, I was just too nervous to get up and ask where the bathroom was. The wind blowing didn't make it easier either, which only got worse as he walked towards me with his infamous smile.

"So, you are just going to make me, huh, Smiley?"

"Smiley? You like calling me that I see," he said as he repeated the pet name I'd given him. "If you only knew,

Noel," he told me, a grim expression on his face. I was unsure what that meant, but I knew one thing. If I didn't get up and find a toilet to squat down on, I'd be wet again like he was before he had changed his clothes. Him being wet from snow. Me being wet from urine. Ugh, I so hate my life right now.

"Better?" he asked me once I'd made it back. I'd learned he was very observant, and as soon as I hissed, he asked, "Noel, love, do you have to use the bathroom?"

"Very much so," I whimpered as he snickered. I was sure my eyes had blinked when he did, but who cares. A girl had to go! "To the left, first door on the right. Now, Noel!" he playfully fussed before I scurried off.

"Was that too hard?"

"No," I said, barely recognizing my own voice once I settled back down.

"Good, because it will get easier the sooner you realize that I'm not going to hurt you or let anything happen to you or these kids. Come on," he demanded in a pushy, yet jovial manner as he led me to the stairwell.

For the next three days, we slowly developed a routine of sorts as he pulled out the food and I made the meals. Nothing fancy since we were reserving the generator by day two, eating sandwiches, chips and fruit. Then, when we were done, we'd find ourselves back in the kitchen, washing dishes together.

The kids and Cookie had their run of the mill all over the

place and Knight allowed them to. Occasionally, he'd warn them to quiet down or stop running, but he could barely keep a straight face when he did. He even watched movies with them while I ducked off to sleep. That generator surely came in handy, I tell you.

By the third day, we were comfortable enough to lay up under each other, talking or not talking at all. And when we said nothing, it felt like our bodies were saying everything as we moved succinctly with each other.

I hadn't thought of fucking Desmond once. Well, I had once or twice, but nothing that made me regret being with Knight. I had no regrets being with him now. In a matter of days, everything I believed to be true about Mason back then was nothing to what I believed to be true now. Mason truly was a place of magic, and it came in the form of Knight Commodore, my modern-day knight in shining armor.

All was well, even when the lights came on, until I heard a voice I knew couldn't be who I thought it was. It just couldn't. I was sure the roads were blocked to delay travel. I figured I was just dreaming I heard the person call my name again and he sounded angry as I flinched. When I did, Knight released me and huffed, "Hold up." That damn Neil was being fucking rude. I could tell as soon as Knight snatched the door open.

"Aye, Noel over? If she is, tell her to get the kids, Cookie, and let's go."

When I saw Knight's fists tightened, I scrambled my ass

up, looked around to cover up, then remembered I was a grown woman. I wasn't naked, but I was in a pair of Knight's sweats and a shirt that was practically swallowing me up.

"And who the hell are you?" I heard him ask, followed by an evil laugh that told me Neil might not be the last man standing.

"Someone you do not want to fuck with," I heard him hiss before I quickly slid underneath his arms with sleep in my eyes, rubbing them.

"Neil, really?" I asked him, not appreciating the way he was looking at the both of us either.

"Damn, Noel," he snickered. "You moved on fast. No more Dezzy?"

"Don't," I warned. Well, really begged him. Until I touched his chest, it didn't seem he was aware of my presence while Neil taunted him by smiling. "That's my brother, the asshole."

This fool mocked me, amping Knight up. I could tell he had a bit of a temper, but who wouldn't when some guy you don't know comes to your spot and behaves the way Neil was. I couldn't wait to get the kids and Cookie out of here so I could go home and give him a piece of my mind.

When Neil told him he didn't play about me, Knight shot back, "Good, 'cause I don't play about her, either." He then leaned down, and in the most tender yet sexy way, placed his full, kissable lips on the top of my head. And if that wasn't enough, he smacked my ass, then whispered, "Thank you for hanging out with me. Let's do this again. Cool?"

"Ah, ye—yeah," was all I could get out as Neil stood there fuming. Serves him right for coming over here as if he didn't have any manners. It was my fault I had no money and his we didn't prepare for snow. If it weren't for Knight, we all would have been in pretty bad shape.

"You sure?" he asked, and for the first time, I think I saw fear. I don't know, maybe I was overthinking it, but he deserved that much from me. No way was I allowing Neil to have his way when he brought his little friend with him.

"I'm sure, Knight. And thank you for everything," I whispered, his eyes smiling just a little as they crinkled. He wasn't too fond of the nickname Smiley, but he'd better get used to it because I think smiling is contagious for us.

11

NOEL LANCASTER

"NEIL! WHY WOULD YOU DO THAT!" I FUSSED AS I SLAMMED the door to our cabin. "He was very kind to us. Gave us food, shelter—"

"And sweets!" the kids tattled as I shook my head. Snitches. Two little freaking snitches in crime except when it came to telling on each other.

"You don't know men like I do, Noel. You're...you're..."

"I'm what?" I was heated he was even trying to justify his actions while blaming me. "I'm what? Not good enough? Pretty enough? Huh?"

"No damn way would I think that, girl," he scoffed. "It's not you. It's them. Damn it, Noel. They are not good enough for you! Not for my sister who deserves everything in life!" he belted in frustration, shutting me down.

"Oh oh," I heard PJ whispered while Paige lifted both brows when we both looked their way.

"Listen, I'm sorry, Noel. I'm sorry you got a bad hand in love when it comes to guys, but it's *not* you. It's always them because you just give and give and men will take, Nollie. And you two," he stopped and said, looking at the kids. "Find something to do in your rooms. Put your stuff away." They moaned and groaned, but once Cookie took off as if she could help them, they followed her.

Once they were going, he sat and sighed, looking worried.

"Nollie, am I making any sense?"

"Neil..."

"And for the record, I wasn't trying to be rude, but Mr. Wakanda stepped up to me like he had a say in why I came to see about my sister," he added with an attitude as soon as the kids came into the living room.

"Mr. Knight is Black Panther, too? Wowwww!" PJ asked with excitement as he stuck his head out the room. "Soooo cool!" he celebrated along with Paige, who yelled, "Wakandaaaa!"

"Oh, God," I groaned. "You all are killing me," I whimpered while I heard a hearty laugh coming from Neil.

"Sorry, sis. I'm saying, though. Dude was standing there like I came for Nakia, face all balled up like we were about to fight to see who would become the King of Wakanda," he said, snickering as he stood.

"I can't wait to tell Mommy that the Black Panther is Auntie Nollie's new boyfriend," Paige rejoiced while PJ started hitting his imaginary drums against his thighs. In no time, they were right back in the living room minding their auntie's business.

"The Black Panther?" Neil's girlfriend, Erin, asked as she came out of the bathroom. "Sorry, long drive. I had to go. Noel, right?" she asked, smiling at Neil like he was the best thing God had ever created.

Ugh. He was right. Men were so full of themselves as Erin practically ignored the rest of our presence until Paige let it be known she had no clue who she was.

"Uncle Neil. Your girlfriend is from Wakanda, too? She just like—" she said then clapped her hands once and lifted them up like the Black Panther did in the movie. "—appeared out of nowhere."

"Huh?" Erin asked no one in particular while it was apparently my turn to bust out laughing. I wanted to high five Paige with her shady little butt, but Neil deserved it.

"Never mind," he told her. "Erin, my annoying, *sneaky* sister Noel and these two are Trouble One and Trouble Two." Strangely, neither protested the nickname he assigned them because they were, in fact, nothing but trouble, but I loved them dearly.

"Pleasure to meet you and you, too. I can vibe with a little bit of trouble myself." I wanted to tell her she drove up with a walking billboard of trouble, but for the most part, Neil was a decent guy. I was actually glad he seemed to be showing some interest in one girl over the past few months. She'd come by the store, but he would whisk her away before we could bombard her with questions.

"What's for breakfast?" he asked, looking at me while I looked at Erin. "You're walking around in his clothes as if you gave him breakfast in bed? I'm just saying," he added with a shrug.

"Go ask your new friend, M'Baku," I told him, calling him a name from one of the men in the movie too since he wanted to be funny. "In fact, I think Knight actually likes you," I replied with a smile, patting his shoulder. "Your face is still intact."

"Did she just call you M'Baku? Wait, I thought your name was Neil?" I heard her ask him as I moseyed on down the hallway to my room. See how quickly karma was kicking Neil's butt?

He could let his girlfriend pick up where I left off when it came to breakfast or whatever it was he felt I was supposed to do for his ass. I had those kids for days, was stuck in a snowstorm and was cooped up with a dog that had to be let out in the snow to go to the bather.

I must have heard about every single girl that hated Paige because some boy liked her the other girls liked while PJ said she was ugly. Then, if it wasn't Paige talking about herself, she was giving Knight all the tea about Desmond. At some point, I really didn't care. I couldn't tell if Knight was a bit amused or not, but even if he decided all we had was what we had now in Mason, he'd done enough to put a smile on my face.

Oh, and in my lady parts, too, that tingled like crazy around him. I was about to go in the room and take care of myself. A girl could only take so much of tall, dark and beautiful.

Yes, Knight Commodore, was a beautiful man inside and outside just like he said I was. Mason was fucking amazing.

Desmond who?

12

NOEL LANCASTER

"He did what?" I squawked, feeling lightheaded as I stood there, blinking.

"You heard me? That freaking liar proposed, Noel. He freaking proposed," Nyla snarled, while Payne yelled in the background he was going to whip his ass as soon as he saw him. "That's right, baby. Beat his ass."

"Are you sure?" I asked, wondering what was going on. Desmond engaged to Cassidy? He's known me since we were in elementary school. Professed his love for me at eleven. Took my virginity at nineteen. Promised me last year that this year would be our year to finally make a go at it, starting with Mason, and now he's freaking engaged?

"That whore is probably pregnant," Nyla spat, really going hard, and while I appreciated that, Cassidy had done nothing to me. It was all me, all my fault for kissing and believing lying lips that now made my heart bleed. "Anyway, enough about that asshole. Who's the hot babe Neil was telling me about? Well, he didn't say hot babe. He said some pussy...or Black Panther," she chuckled, while I rolled my eyes. "Neil's such a girl sometimes. He's the pussy."

"Ah, damn," Payne said in the background. "I'm out of here so you can talk trash about my brother-in-law. I don't want any damn parts of that. But tell Nollie, I got her. Desmond's ass is going down," he added as Nyla agreed.

"I love that guy, Nollie. Whew!" she released in my ear as I pulled the cell back and started at it.

"So, this guy, what's the story with him? Kids? Wife? Side chicks? Bitches on the prowl?" Nyla asked, snickering at her silly behind husband.

"Let's see," I replied, grinning as I mentally went through each question in my head. "No kids. No wife I know of if the left ring finger matters these days. Maybe a few side chicks who haven't revealed themselves. And as for bitches, I can't blame them, sis!" I squealed as I fell back on my bed. thinking about Knight.

His smell, his touch, his presence alone. He was just huge. I mean larger than life as soon as he showed up. He effortlessly commanded my attention and he received it, too. The kids loved him, welcoming him in effortlessly while those snots told my business.

"And your children are snitches. He already knows about Desmond."

“What do you mean?” she asked, gasping. “Listen, Noel. We never tell the new guy about the old guy. Abort mission. Abort. The. Mission.”

“I didn’t. Your children did and *neither* of them are my guys,” I reminded her.

“I can’t believe I’m missing this! Payne! We need to go to Mason now!” I don’t know what he said, but whatever it was made Nyla gasp.

“This man,” she whispered excitedly. “Noel, don’t overthink and also don’t be mad.”

“About what?”

“I sort of, uh, sent a suitcase with Neil and Erin full of a few outfits I think you’d actually look cute in.” Great, I’m twenty-one being dressed by my sister to go on imaginary dates since no one has even asked me out. Knight’s probably pissed off, so that wasn’t even an option. “Are you still there?” she practically yelled in my ear as I pulled it away.

“Nyla, enjoy your husband while I’m constantly teased by your kids. Those outfits will come back the same way you packed them. “On that note, good bye,” I sang, hanging up on her. Everyone was doing everything they wanted from my parents to Neil to Desmond and now Nyla with no input from me. I just wished everyone would leave me alone.

I practically buried myself under my quilt, threw my headphones on and listened to Beyonce’s station on Shazam until I felt off to sleep. I didn’t even realize how tired I was until Paige hopped into my bed and pinched my nose.

"Stop, Paige. Go away, please."

"Okay, I will. I will just tell Mr. Knight you want him to leave," she said when I shot up, snatching the quilt back. "Knight? He's here. Like right now? In our cabin?" I asked, as Paige nodded her head up and down quickly with a Kool-Aid smile.

"Yep, and guess what? We have presents," she said, crawling in my lap. "Oh, boy. Auntie Nollie, if you want to keep the Blank Panther, you got to do better than this," she said, pushing my hair out of my face. "And Mommy usually wears something sexy in bed. What is this?" she asked.

I had stripped down to nothing but my boy shorts and a long-sleeved, fitted top. The usual stuff I wore to bed.

"How about you be six and not worry about what I'm wearing to bed. Then go tell Mr. Knight I'm coming."

"Fine," she giggled, sliding off my lap. "But hurry up. Uncle Neil's face looks like this," she said, poking her lips out with a creased forehead. "I don't think he likes you playing with Mr. Knight, but I think he's cute," she whispered. "So, put on anything but this," her little fast butt told me before she waltzed right on out my room as if would take advice from a six-year-old.

Ten minutes later, guess what I did?

I took advice from a six-year-old, and from the way he was looking at me, it worked. It freaking worked.

13

KNIGHT COMMODORE

"AYE," I SAID, LETTING QUEEN IN, WHO CAME BEARING anything but gifts. In fact, it was a thick file that she all but dangled with her lip twisted. "Everything cool? Didn't know you were coming up," I told her, after being out all day.

Instead of allowing Noel's brother to bring the worse out in me since I wasn't giving up that easily anyway, I went back into town and decided to do some shopping. I hadn't had a chance before I came up, so then was a good time to do that. I even located a pretty chill Irish Bar that sold a decent beer and cabbage beef pie that had me stuffed. To walk it off, I made sure I went inside of damn near every store, picking up not only things for my family, but Noel and the children, too. Yeah, Noel's ass had my mind gone.

I even picked up a Christmas tree and decorations since we never had a chance to decorate their tree a few nights ago.

If her brother thought that stunt he pulled this morning would work, he was going to fucking lose it when I showed up unannounced and prepared not to leave unless Noel was on my arm.

"Want to tell me about this before I open this up?" I asked her as she followed me to the kitchen where there were a few bottles of wine in the refrigerator. My social media stroll told me she loved Takari Plum wine, so I grabbed not one but two of those. One would be for tonight, and the other one would be for later before we left Mason. I guess you can tell I was on something else, feeling lighter, happier and shit. I can't explain it, I just was.

"Just know that whatever you want to do next, consider it done. Even if it's nothing. You know...until you figure it out," she said with concern on her face as I motioned for her to follow me to the living room. Whatever this was, was serious, so we needed to sit down.

"I'm sorry, Knight," she told me softly, taking a seat. "It just wasn't something I could do over the phone or text."

"Damn," I said lowly, sitting down and slowly opening the envelope.

Once I pulled out the contents, I stopped and looked her way suspiciously. Rayelle was full of shit when it came to the games she played about a relationship she thought we were in, but these weren't photos of her with a man. These were photos of her with Cleo, my fucking mother.

"So, uh, they're kicking it and shit?" I asked her, rubbing

the top of my head as I processed what I was looking at. I could tell they were from different days based on their clothes. Some early morning, some at night. "What's up, Queen?" I asked, really not up for it, but fuck it. She was here and I was hot. Gone was my great fucking mood just like that.

"There's more in the folder, Knight. The bank statements."

Bank statements? I was praying Queen wasn't about to have me do or say something I could never come back from. I was very familiar with our books. Used to do them myself when we started out a few years ago until King took that over. But the more I looked at them, the more the pattern stuck out to me. They were all line items to one ad firm, one I had never heard of. Scooting up, I took a closer look.

"Ad Mates?" I asked her. "Who are they, and why are we paying them so much money every month, Queen?"

"Our mother," she said, sighing. "Ad Mates is our mother's company, and the person submitting those for approval, according to the audit we ran is, unfortunately, Rayelle. And before you say anything," she told me when I grunted. "My legal team is looking into it. Somehow, when we pay out, we are not cutting checks to Ad Mates. So, the middleman is really—"

"Rayelle," I answered for her, fuming on the inside. After everything I accepted from her because at one time in my life, she stopped me from being in a fucked-up place mentally, and this bitch is stealing from me?

"We think our mother is blackmailing her, though, Knight," she whispered with misty eyes. I don't know why, though. I been told her Cleo wasn't shit.

"Handle it," is all I said, deciding to not allow any of that bullshit to mess up my night. No way was I about to let those two motherfuckers mess up what I could have with Noel. Just that quickly, I thought of Miss Reynolds. She would want me happy. Hell, I want to be happy, so this was the answer to getting them both out of my life.

"I'm so sorry, Knight. I don't understand why our mother just won't do right by us."

"Naw, we are not doing any of that tonight. Queen Commodore is a beast. This is nothing. Just let it be an eye opener that blood don't make a bitch family. Character does. Shut the account down now that disperses those payments. Send Rayelle a resignation letter advising her this is her last day and because I'm feeling quite generous, have a severance letter drawn up with clear instructions that she is to never come even across the street from CE before I handle her my damn self," I told her, standing up and tossing that bullshit on the sofa.

"Where are you going?" she shot up in a panic. I don't know why when she had what she needed which was for me to tell her what to do.

I stopped and sighed, wondering if I should keep it real with Queen. Noel was my escape, my one time in life where I could be happy and it not be about money or a motherfucker thinking they are getting over on me. Hell, she didn't care about my money, still trying to pay me back for some damn groceries. When I looked at her, I knew I had to. Queen was worried and she'd been fucked up all night if I didn't tell her, so I did.

"I have plans tonight. And if it goes well, you just might have someone your brother will actually consider his girl," I told her as she leaped up and screamed. "Damn, Queen. All of that?" I chuckled as she hugged me.

"I—I. Did you? Did I? Wait, what's her name?" she asked me, pulling her cell out. I wasn't sure what was funnier, Queen forgetting all about this stunt her mother pulled to prove I was right all of these years or her immediately going into detective mode about who magically had placed a spell on me. Hell, it had to be a spell because what Queen told me just a week ago would have sent me to a dark place. I was there for a second, but again, I had something to look forward to. My new coping skill was making sure I kept Noel around for as long as she would let me.

Hell, anytime I thought of Noel, dark couldn't even exist at the same place at the same time. Even in her most awkward moments, Noel was damn near perfect to me. She led with her heart and I messed with that. If I wasn't allowing her punk ass brother to stop me, I most certainly wasn't allowing Rayelle and Cleo.

"Thank you for having my back, sis. And her name is Noel. Noel Lancaster," I told her with a grin. "As for Cleo, guess what? Let her keep what she has. If money is more valuable than a relationship with me, what sense does it make holding on to something that serves me no purpose?"

"Who the hell are you, and where is my brother?"

"Stop playing, Queen," I chuckled, leaning down and pulling her into a hug.

"Un-uh. I need to do some investigating and now," she said, touching my forehead with the back of her hand. "Dang, no fever."

"You wild, but I'm serious. It's time to let go and start over. Do the family thing and make sure we add Mason to it every year."

"Every year?"

"Get on it. That's an order, Queen. I'm out."

14

NOEL LANCASTER

ONCE KNIGHT SHOWED UP, ERIN HAD STRICT ORDERS TO PUSH him right on back out there. It took no time for Neil to tell Nyla who put operation "Nyla, Fix My Life" into motion, employing her substitute.

Neil told him if he wanted to see me, it had to be a date or nothing at all, and with ease, Knight gave me a wink and told me he would give me an hour because we were going on a date.

Too bad that backfired on Neil, but now I was wondering if maybe I had bit off more than I could chew. I was okay with my Cinderella in Mason being over, but between Knight and Neil, this episode was far from over.

"I don't like it all," Neil growled while his girlfriend told me to stay still. "Women. Things you all do to make a man like you or to get him jealous..." he said and stopped once he remembered Erin was right there as if she wasn't a woman.

"Not you, babe. Chill," he told her, raising his hands in surrender while I watched him destroy himself minding my business.

"Oh, I will tonight. *All night*. I'm going to chill so hard, you will need a few blankets it will so chill in here," she replied with a fake smile on her face, tilting her head.

"Erin..." he said, sighing as he stood up, almost begging with his eyes. My brother, Neil? Begging? "I'll be in the room," he said, quickly getting out of our way.

"I'd never thought I'd see the day," I mumbled.

"The crazy thing is, he's right," she whispered, then snickered as she looked over her shoulder. "The key is to always remember you have nothing to lose. They do. Don't give them the playbook to play you. Just go with it and be yourself."

"Like now...wearing this?"

"Hey, I'm just following orders. Now, be still." I wasn't sure how Nyla was able to get Erin on board so fast. Especially since I'd just really met her, but oh well. She had a boyfriend, I didn't, so she had to be doing something right.

"Ouch!" I fussed as she plucked a stubborn eyelash.

"Sorry. Almost done," she replied with a tight-lipped smile, silently apologizing. "Your eyebrows and cheekbones are to die for, but these eyelashes, girl..."

"Are just eyelashes," I replied, squinting my eyes. I

wanted to cry so bad but couldn't or Neil would be sure to remind me why I shouldn't be doing this anyway.

"I beg to differ, but since you won't allow me to add some lashes, at least let me get these together before I finish up with your eye liner and eye shadow. Oh, and your skin is amazing," she cooed excitedly as she stood back as if she was a proud mama bear.

She was definitely Neil's type. Very fashionable, shapely and the kind that smiled with her eyes with butterscotch skin and long tresses that swung effortlessly as if the wind were following her around. Then her button nose coupled with heart-shaped lips made her America's darling who could do no wrong. She could easily land on a runway. She wasn't a Cassidy, who looked borderline plastic to me with her almost too perfect body, but Erin's aura and body were definitely head turners.

"Oww," I yelped.

"Almost done," she sang. "Pain is power."

Pain is power? Is this the crap girls tell other girls? Pain is me getting knocked on my butt when skiing. All I have left is a sore butt. Damn, my night was doomed.

"And don't pay Neil any mind. Between you and I, he's pretty stoked about this date. He wants to kill this Desmond guy, but I say he's done you a favor."

"It's just one date, and I think Knight's just being nice," I told her when we heard a light knock on the door.

"I didn't see nice, Noel. Even when you came out here in

your mountain gear tights or whatever you call those. Now, loosen up. That's got to be him," she said, standing back and giving me the thumbs up. "Well, hello there," she said, but it didn't matter. Knight didn't look her way, not even once, yet he spoke as he came inside as I stood there speechless.

"He's staring," Erin whispered as if Knight couldn't hear it. "A lot. Oh my God, Noel. You look..."

"Amazing," he finished. "Beyond amazing," he said, this time pulling a bouquet of roses from behind his back. Yellow ones, too. "For friendship."

"And that's all it better be," Neil grumbled when he stomped into the living room as Erin and I shot him a look.

"What? I don't know this guy," he fussed lowly while the kids practically pushed me to the side, giving Knight a hug. Cookie was excited, barking and running us in circles.

"Well, good evening, Princess Paige, and the all-knowing PJ, the Wizard." I so forgot how many times Knight watched the *Wizard of Oz* with them, sliding in lessons about life in the most simplistic way. Knight could barely keep his eyes opened as they huddled up on the sofa, watching it on their tablet, grateful he made them forget all about that nasty snowstorm a few nights ago.

"Yes!" PJ celebrated, loving the fact that Knight called him the Wizard.

"Thank you, Mr. Knight. You always know how to make a girl smile," Paige giggled, batting her eyes

"What the heck?" Neil barked. "Alright, you two. Time for

bed. And you," he said, looking at Knight as he huffed and puffed. "Take care of my sister."

"Taking care of her is all I want to do," he said with ease as I sniffed the roses.

"Let me find a vase and put these in water," Erin offered. "Go on now," she playfully fussed, pushing me towards the coat rack and handing me my scarf. "Just temporary until you two get somewhere warm inside. If you know what I mean."

"Erin, you too?" Neil asked her.

"Girl, bye, before this becomes a long holiday for your brother," Erin told me, taking the flowers out of my hands and nudging me along. "Now, remember, wait for him to do everything and bat your eyes, too, girl. Just like your niece. I have no clue who raised that child," she whispered, nudging me along as Knight chuckled, pretending like he didn't hear her.

"Erin!"

By the time we walked down the driveway, I was crying on the inside. These thigh-high leather boots were killing as I pressed a smile on my face. If he only knew how I wish I could throw on some boots or my Timberlands. Yet, I did exactly what Erin said, lightly batting my eyes as he opened the truck door and helped me in.

Once he got inside, he leaned over and said, "The boots are alright, but next time, just rock with something you're more comfortable in. More you,"

"Oh," I said, clearing my throat. I didn't realize it was that obvious. "I was trying something new," I told him, which he still seemed to appreciate as his eyes traveled up my legs to my face as I crinkled my nose. The eggshell and gold turtleneck sweater dress made me warm, but I couldn't lie. It did give me a tad bit more ass and hips than I knew existed. Then I wore gold hooped earrings that dangled freely since my dread locs were pulled up tightly in a bun.

"What would you have liked to have worn?"

"Honestly?"

"Yes, honestly," he asked, studying me as if I were some sort of puzzle with intense eyes that made me fan myself as he laughed. "I'm being for real, Noel. What would have preferred?

"A pair of Kate Moss wedge boots or my Timbs, but not with this dress, though. God, no," I confessed, unsure if that was a mistake or not.

"Tonight, you get a pass, but after that, don't pretend with me. I take being authentic very seriously," he told me and I could tell he was serious. Very serious as I touched the passenger door latch, wondering if I should just end this now.

"Don't play with me, Noel. All I'm saying is be yourself. Being who you are is what pulled me in, connected me to you, made me want to fuck with you harder. Clothes and all that name brand bullshit is just that. All bullshit. Don't work hard to be like anyone else. Don't let anyone else make you do something you don't want to do, cool?"

"Y—yeah."

"Noel, love," he said, this time with a softness in his voice. A softness that made me wonder if it even came from him. Not that he couldn't be because I'd seen it with the kids if they were fighting and one was crying. He'd ease right on in and help them settle their differences, ending it with an apology and hug.

"Noel? I don't like repeating myself, love," he told me, turning my head his way delicately by my chin with his index finger. "I like you... a lot. Remember that," he said, cranking up the truck and pulling off. "The you I met...the you I'm falling for."

Oh shit. I took a deep breath and nodded, then remembered he liked words. "I like you too... a lot."

"Good," was all he said as he slid his hand into mine before he lifted it and kissed the back of my hand. The entire ride, I was a ball of nerves, but he did his best to make me comfortable. I could tell and I appreciated that.

I couldn't help but stare his way and feel all giddy inside. Knight Commodore was anything but common, yet he liked tomboy, Plain Jane Noel Lancaster. I was about to burst on the inside, eager to text Nyla a play by play, but he made it clear that tonight there were no cell phones. Even locked his in the glove compartment before we got out.

As we pulled up to the Red Lounge, I got excited. The

Red Lounge was the go-to spot in Mason. Especially on the nights they played karaoke and had spoken word.

Coincidentally enough, our color schemes matched as he wore a tan and cream Balenciaga sweater and tanned jeans that hung loosely around his hips, emphasizing his bow legged stance. His leather coat was Balenciaga, too, and while he'd just lectured me about name brand, I could tell that's just how he dressed. Not who he was since I'd suspected from the first night he was definitely rich. I didn't want to pry, and still wouldn't, but Knight was no one's employee.

And even if he was, he didn't carry himself like one and that alone turned me on. Not his money, his attire. Especially since I had no clue what he did or how much money he made. That didn't matter to me. What mattered is he was taking the time to get to know the real me and making me actually like myself.

"Did I tell you that I like your hair better when you let it hang down loose?" he mentioned, as he took my coat and bent down, pressing his mouth against my ear.

"I don't think so." Shit, his body felt good against mine as he slid his arm around my waist.

"But keeping it up tonight means I can do more of this," he whispered, nuzzling his nose against my ear and neck as I shivered. "Fucking sexy, Noel. Let me get us inside so I can sit my ass down before I don't get pass the first date.

"Whatever," I squealed lowly. He was going to get more than a first date if my center that thumped erratically had anything to do with it. Just that quickly, I forgot all about these uncomfortable ass boots.

"Oh and your niece and nephew are right," he said, chuckling as he sat down slowly as he took me in.

"Oh, yeah. And what's that?" I replied coyly as we walked hand and hand towards the entrance.

"That you need new friends. Apparently, the last one you had sucked. I'm glad he did. Remind me to send him a gift of appreciation when I tell him all of that shit is fucking dead." He stopped when he said it, looking at me with intense eyes. Warm cedar brown eyes that made me want to take him back to the truck and sit on his face. Nyla was right. I needed this date.

"Dead?" I all but whispered.

"Dead, dead. Hands clapping and picture snapping...at his funeral dead."

Oh my God. There was definitely some kind of magic in the air. Mason was surprising me on every hand, starting with this man who devoured me with his eyes, causing my stomach to flutter.

"Well shit then, dead," I said and chuckled, as he opened the door and waited for me to walk inside.

15

KNIGHT COMMODORE

ONCE I GOT THEM TO ALLOW ME TO TAKE NOEL ON A DATE, I hit Queen up, asking her for help. I'd never dated a woman before, truthfully. I'd done things I was already doing for myself and they had come along for the ride, but with them in mind, hell no!

"Are you sure about tonight?" Queen asked me with a confused and concerned look on her face. "I just laid something heavy on you hours ago and you're smiling as if you don't have a care in the world."

"Shit, because I don't. Rayelle's a fucking bird and Cleo is...well, Cleo is Cleo. It's money, Queen. If that's all she wants, she got it. In fact, I forgive her. She made it easy I told you."

I was still wondering if I'd actually forgiven her. I said it, though, so it was at least step one to actually trying to do it. Noel was exactly what I needed as a distraction. I liked who I was when I was around her. It was why I had been all up in her face and space since I'd met her. In three days, she made me want to be better and not in terms of getting more money. I was a master at that. Just being a better person period. Doing shit out of my heart and not obligation.

"And what exactly do you know about her? I did my research and—"

"Yo, Queen. Not now," I chuckled, shaking my head as I brushed my hair. Queen was all in my room when all I did was call her and asked her what was something nice to do for a girl I was trying to impress. Can you believe that? Me, Knight Commodore, trying to impress a girl. Fucking nuts.

"Knight, do you know who you are? Who we are? If Rayelle could do it, someone I at least thought loved you at one point, what else would you expect from me when three days later, I pop up and you're grinning and shit like you just popped your first cherry."

"Can I just be normal for once, Queen?" There, I said it. I was far from normal, but it didn't mean I didn't want to be. I went from being a reckless, angry kid to a well composed, well to do, grown ass man who happens to be a millionaire. "Like, treat me like your brother. Your brother who's playing catch up, being that little boy that didn't get to date. Didn't get to ask a girl's parents out, Queen. Do you know I've never done that shit before?" I asked her, my chest heaving up and down from her pushing my buttons, forcing me to think about who I really was.

Shit, Noel was worried about not being good enough for me, but damn it if it wasn't the other way around. She was pure and I was tainted, tainted and cold, yet she still wanted to get to know me. Know me and actually not wanting a fucking thing but to lay up and chill with me. I'd never had that. Never. Not until Noel.

"Okay, I can do that," she whispered more to herself before she looked in my eyes, cupping my cheek. "You're right, Knight. You should get a chance to be normal since you allowed me and King to have that. I'll back off...for now."

"Shoot, period. Don't be running my girl off."

"Your girl? Un-uh, I got to tell King about this," she said, smiling as she pinched my cheek, making me feel like a little boy. "Your heart is good, Knight. Everything you did, you did for us. Can't nobody judge you for that. Now go, and don't be so pushy. Everyone doesn't work for you and everyone's not afraid of you."

"Yeah, yeah," I told her, leaning down and giving her a kiss on the cheek. "Follow me out. I don't need your nosey ass snooping through my cabin."

Now as I sat in front of Noel, I still didn't feel normal, but I did feel better. This new feeling was...nice.

"Did I tell you how much I enjoyed myself tonight?" I

asked her with her feet on my lap. I know, I know, but I couldn't help it. After she winced a few times, I slipped those damn boots off and propped both of her feet on my lap. I gave her, I assumed, the most intense and mind-blowing foot rub as she sat across from me, making those faces as she crinkled her nose. At least she'd stopped blinking those eyes, which I finally told her I noticed she'd done before she made me think she was crazy.

"I think so," she hissed. That shit was like music to my ears, but then she groaned, and I did, too. I was ready to pull one of her cute, little toes in my mouth and suck that motherfucker. "I'm so embarrassed. Gosh, did I really just groan out loud?"

"So, I did, too," I chuckled, then moved a tad bit closer. When I did, her thighs were now across my thigh. She smelled so fucking good, too. I was full after eating about fifteen wings, an order of snow crabs and grilled corn on the cob. The Red Lounge was something I had to look into. I was messing with that atmosphere hard.

"I can go for some dessert," I told her lowly, easing my hand up and down her leg as she shivered. "Want me to stop?" I asked her.

"No!" she replied quickly, then caught herself. "I mean, no. This feels good."

"It does," I said, studying the goose bumps on her cinnamon-colored skin that smelled like cinnamon, too. I wanted to ask her if her pussy tasted like cinnamon, but the date was going too well to fuck it up like that. She was no Rayelle, and because she wasn't, I wouldn't dare treat her as such. Rubbing her alone made my dick hard but being in her presence was the ultimate reward.

"A penny for your thoughts?" she asked me and I hollered.

"So you got your little clutch tonight, and now you want my pennies, too?"

"Knight," she playfully grunted as she lightly popped my hand. "Just remind me to pay you back as soon as I get back to my cabin tonight."

"Who says I'm taking you back? Your brother? I think I want to keep you," I told her, refusing to look in her eyes. If I did, my soul might just break if she even attempted to reject me.

I could tell she felt the shift when she jumped and out of nowhere declared, "I want to sing. Sit and watch my clutch. Don't be stealing my pennies now."

"Girl, gone now," I told her, blushing like a little-ass boy. I hoped she didn't notice as I watched her walk away and signed up to perform. Tonight's winner would perform against the winners who had won earlier this week for some kind of grand prize.

When it was her turn, she eased up on stage. I could tell she was nervous, but when searched and found me, she waved. I nodded my head as encouragement as she smiled before she grabbed the microphone.

"Good evening, everyone. My name's Noel," she said, and a few men whistled. Immediately, I looked around to let them know to chill. She wasn't my *girl* girl, but she was here with me. "And tonight, I want to perform for a special someone who is like a dream come true to me. Some really special I mess with hard. I think he's stuck with me," she said, using my words like she was some little gangster as I blushed. Noel better calm her scary ass down. She just didn't know what stuck was until I showed her.

She then leaned over and whispered what song she wanted them to play. It had to be a Christmas song, too, in order to win the prize. I hoped she was about to do something cute, you know, something I could get in to like "Gee Whiz, it's Christmas". But if she chose something like "What Do the Lonely Do at Christmas", I had an answer for that. She was looking at him when she looked at me. Her ass was about to do me, the fucking Knight of her life. Yeah, you caught that, huh?

When she started, I closed my eyes since the song was unfamiliar, but it didn't matter, though, because once she started, I could tell she was singing to me.

"Baby, if you've got to go away. I don't think I can take the pain. Won't you stay another day. Oh, don't leave me alone like this. Don't say it's the final kiss. Won't you stay another day," she belted, her eyes locked in with mine.

When it got good to her, she swayed then took a step down. She belted out each note like some high school girl singing to her crush. When she got to me, she took my hand and all as we began to dance. The crowd went crazy, too, but what went crazier was this fluttering shit in my stomach. I don't know what it was, but damn it if didn't keep on fluttering. Old girl had Knight Commodore about to piss on himself I was so nervous.

"Stay another day," she whispered as she held the note, her face against mine as she tricked me into slow dancing.

By the time the song was over, the crowd asked for an encore. I didn't oblige them, though. Instead, I lifted Noel's ass up and carried her to our table where I sat her down.

"Whew," she said, her chest heaving up and down while I bent down to slip her boots on. The energy was thick and tense, so tense, she could probably get me to say something outlandish like I think I love her or some shit.

"How was I?" she asked once I stood up and took her in. Shit, if I wasn't in love, I was close to it, and I think she knew it, too.

"Stay another day?" I asked instead.

"It's a Christmas song, Knight."

"You sure, Noel, love?" I leaned down and asked her as my lips grazed against hers. "Or are you propositioning me? I like propositions."

"Well," she whispered against my lips. "What about both?"

"Then I accept," I told her, gathering our things and getting us up out of there. I learned some white boys sang that damn song, but I can't lie. I was about to add that to my playlist, so each time I thought of her, I could rewind time in mind and spend it with her.

16

KNIGHT COMMODORE

"YOU'RE SHIVERING," I WHISPERED AS I LED HER INTO THE cabin, the fireplace already lit, awaiting our arrival.

"Cold maybe," she replied as I heard a nervousness in her voice. Or maybe a lie. "Okay, I am lying," she quickly confirmed. "I'm sorry, especially since we agreed for me to be honest. I'm very nervous."

"The only difference is now it's just us. No kids, no Cookie, no lounge full of people, but nothing changes, Noel. I just want to spend time with you and only you. Can we do that?" I asked her, tilting her chin up so she not only heard me, but felt me, too.

Besides, I wasn't hard up for pussy by a long shot, but I'd do just about anything to get her to stay. I knew I needed her to anyway when I felt the money I'd spent on her back in my coat pocket. Guess she slipped it in there with her stubborn ass. I wanted to check her about that before we got here, but now all I wanted was for Noel to let me in her world.

"Won't you get comfortable," I told her as she snickered like she was shy. Too late for that. She made me get up and dance in front of all of those people. Now she was about to do what I told her to do.

"Take this dress off," I told her. All that snickering and smiling had dissipated immediately. "Naw, take it off now. Go ahead. I've already seen you now. Tell me I'm lying," I told her before I picked her up again.

"Knight!" she screamed as I tickled her mercilessly. "Knight, please, please. I'm about to cry," she groaned in between little smacks against my back.

I felt like a kid all over again. That was because of Noel. I was going to keep going and going until she agreed to stop playing with me before I felt my cell buzzing. I let it go to voicemail, but when it buzzed again, I decided to give in and put her down.

"I'm so going to get you," she told me, plopping down all winded on my sofa. And damn it if she didn't look like she belonged right there.

I fished it out of my pocket and saw it was Queen calling. "Stay right there," I told her as I headed upstairs. I was going to find something for her to slip on to prove I wasn't trying to have sex. Besides, it was her that mind fucked me tonight. I pray no one caught that on live, wondering if that was why Queen was calling.

By the time I answered, she had hung up. Right before I could call her back, a text message came in. It was a screenshot.

"Foreclosure?" I whispered. confused as hell. I tapped the screen twice and then spread the image just a little to see who was in foreclosure. "Lancaster Pet Suites and Kennel. Damn."

That explained it all when she told me why her parents wanted to stay back in Jonestown instead of coming up to Mason. I wasn't surprised Queen couldn't chill and mind her business, but this time was the one time I was appreciative she didn't.

Their store was up for auction by the first of the year. That meant it could be sold for a measly eighty thousand dollar loan in front of everyone on the courthouse steps as if that wasn't their life, their foundation, their family legacy. I understood what that meant, so I decided to do something I had hoped Noel nor her parents would never find out I did. I didn't want to humiliate them. I just wanted to help them.

Pay it off. Send the title to them FedEx and do it anonymously.

Once I did, I placed my cell on Do Not Disturb. I went to my closet, pulled down a quilt, and grabbed two pillows. This place had all these bedrooms, but we discovered we loved sleeping on the floor or on the sofa in front of the fireplace.

After I changed into a pair of sweats and a t-shirt, I

grabbed one of my shirts I was sure was large enough to cover Noel's fine ass. She was always saying she wasn't working with much, but I had two hands full of ass tonight in the Red Lounge, which was more than enough for me.

By the time I came downstairs and looked Noel's way, I halted, close to stumbling as she stood there naked as the day she was born. Her breasts were a delight to see as her chest heaved up and down as she panted, I assumed, from fear. The silhouette of her hips made me harden like steel as my eyes traveled down to her pussy. Pussy that was exactly how I liked mine with just a little hair on it.

"I want you to be sure, Noel. I *need* you to be sure," I released quietly as I walked towards her. I rested my forehead against her forehead as my exhale became her inhale, my heartbeat now her heartbeat, my soul now her soul and the only thing that could stop me was her. Little old her.

"I—I'm sure."

"I'm glad. Thank you for choosing me," I told her, rubbing both of her shoulders as she continued to shiver. "I won't hurt you, Noel love. I wouldn't dare."

I pulled her in and wrapped my arms around her torso, my nose tickling from the smell of guess what? You know it —cinnamon.

"Your hair smells delicious, Noel love. I wonder what else smells good," I probed. When I did, she fidgeted just a little as I dragged my hands down her arms and took her by both hands.

"I don't know what to do next?" she admitted, swallowing hard.

"Come," I told her softly, leading her to the fireplace where I then spread out the soft lambskin rug on the floor. I'd dropped that shit like it was hot when I first peeped my girl standing in all her glory like an unwrapped package, ready to be unwrapped even more.

As I lowered her on the rug, the flickering of the fire made her glow, her hair splayed across the rug as I took her in. I could barely breathe, wondering how I had done that before our paths and souls had crossed.

The smell of cinnamon coupled with the smell of her essence created a high like none other as I dropped to my knees and pushed her thighs open to each side. Her pussy opened up, too, blooming like a flower just for me. That shit was beautiful. Beautiful and slick as one touch of my finger just slightly in between the folds of her love caused her to groan.

"You hear that?" I asked her as I played in her wetness. I liked that shit as I pushed her legs back and lapped up everything she'd supplied like a river of love coating my tongue and throat. It was sweet, beyond sweet. I wanted to drown in it and overdose on her sweet release as she came for me effortlessly while tears escaped her eyes.

"Noel, love," I groaned, nuzzling my nose in that pussy before I pecked her asshole and she squirmed. I could tell she was shocked, but there was no need to be. There wasn't a part of her I didn't want to taste, suck and feel as I spread her ass cheeks and slowly licked from her asshole all the way up to her pussy. Then back down repeatedly until she released for me yet again.

"Oh my...fuck...Knight, baby....shit," she cried out, as her back arched. That shit was beautiful as I rose with her, and just when she started to come down, I took her by her throat and slid up in my pussy. Y'all heard exactly what I said. That was a done deal. Desmond the fuck who?

"Shit," I grunted, feeling her tight walls struggle to receive me as I dipped in and out with just the head as I took her by her mouth. "Pussy already good. Fuck, Noel," I groaned against her lips before I pulled her bottom lip in and sucked on it like I did that pussy. She started working those motherfucking hips, her pussy being all greedy for the dick. "You want this, huh?"

"Yes, baby. Please...I...I...Shit! Who are you?" she cried out before she answered her own question. "Fuck, Knight. Oh shit, oh shit. Knight, baby. Shit, Knight."

"Yes. That's me, Noel love," I told her as I worked that pussy over. I guess it got really good to her when, all of a sudden, she wrapped her legs around my waist, then started riding me like she owned the dick. Shit, I guess she did.

By morning time, I was convinced Mason was more than a place of magic. It was starting to become a place of love. It had to be since Noel Lancaster was my new addiction, my new drug. She came in and started peeling back those hard layers formed around my heart. I wasn't sure how it had happened but going back to a time where she didn't exist in my world would feel like a slow death. That I'm sure of, and I'd be damned if I allowed anyone to tell me she didn't belong in my world and I not in hers.

17

NOEL LANCASTER

WHEN I RETURNED TO THE CABIN THE FOLLOWING EVENING, I was sure I was about to do the walk of shame. Yet, I was met with an empty cabin with a note that they'd gone into town to listen to Christmas carols. Thank God they had because my body was literally racked with pain...but in a good way. Two words. Knight Commodore. Whew!

There were no words to describe how I felt when I was around him. Hell, even when I wasn't around him. I know people say that love at first sight is not possible, but tell that to my heart that roared like a raging ocean. It was insane, which made me question what I thought I even had all those years with Desmond because he couldn't even compare.

In a matter days, Knight had done that and more just by being him. I could tell he had a good heart, a heart I could tell had been broken. Especially when he would sit in deep thought, totally tuning out from the world Well, all of the world except me. If I even moved or flinched just a little, he was on it, asking me what was wrong or where I was going.

"This girl," I said and giggled, seeing Nyla call me on FaceTime. If I didn't know any better, I would have sworn she had a tracker on my whereabouts. Good thing I hadn't disrobed, but this was going to have to be a quick one. I needed to get in and out of the shower before Neil came home, inspecting me like he was an inspector general.

"Yes, sister?" I said and smiled as her eyes stretched wide. I already knew what was coming, but unlike her kids, I wasn't offering up any information. I wanted to initially but I swear keeping to myself made it feel sacred, whole, pure even.

"Well alright then!" she screamed, laughing and tossing her head back. "I don't even have to ask, bitch. You've been marked!"

"I have?" I shot up and ran to the mirror.

"Un-huh," she sang and danced, swerving her hips until Payne told her to sit her butt down. They looked like they were sitting in beach chairs and the sun looked amazing in the background where it met the ocean line. "You are such a whore, Noel. A whore, but I love it! I knew Mason was what you needed. And from what Erin told me, he's tall and built like fucking Ford! Built to ride and built to last!"

"Oh, God," I said, wondering what I needed to do to cover these up.

Nyla might be excited, and even Erin, but Neil was really

about to flip out. He truly despised Desmond, so Knight was just getting the aftermath of that energy and first. Now the hate would be official because he fucked Neil's baby sister after he'd been warned. I sort of told Knight that and his reply was, "He told me to take care of his sister. I did that shit, Noel love. Or naw?"

He ass was so cocky, but I loved it. I really did. When we were finally done, I couldn't get up fast with my legs feeling like noodles after being pushed, pulled, lifted and wrapped around Knight's beautiful, sun-kissed chocolate body. Whew, that man was all man.

"What should I do?" I asked her, panicking.

"Neil will be fine, but a quick remedy is an ice cube. Stick it on there and let it rest. If that doesn't help, just wear a scarf, or better yet, nothing. You're a grown woman, Noel. Besides, he's screwing Erin."

"Now you know we both know that he has double standards," I groaned when I heard someone pounding on the door. "What the hell? Did you hear that?"

"Girl, probably my rowdy behind kids," she chuckled. "I want all the details later when we both get back. Don't tell them I called. I'm hiding from them," she snickered, disconnecting the line. I couldn't even get out of the room fast enough before they were knocking again.

"Why are you knocking so freaking hard?" I yelled, opening the door, almost losing it when I saw that it was fucking Desmond.

When I tried to slam it in his face, he halted it with his hand. "Noel, baby. Just listen, okay? We need to talk, like really talk," he said like the spineless, conniving snake he was.

"One, I'm not your baby, and listen to what? Your great news about your engagement?" I snarled, fighting hard to keep my emotions at bay. "I know already, so goodbye."

"Who cares about that stupid girl, Noel Elaine Lancaster," he hissed, bumping my chest as he pushed me in the house before he slammed the door. "You think I give a damn about Cassidy when I see you trotting around town like some...some whore wearing this? When have you ever even worn some shit like this?" he growled before he grabbed me by my chin and lifted my head. "Passion marks? Since when, Noel?"

I was pissed. Too fucking pissed as he continued to interrogate me, pointing his finger in my face like I'd run off and had an affair. We weren't married. Matter of fact, we weren't even dating. And never mind how good he looked or how good he smelled, he was still a lying asshole who was dealing with a different Noel. Fuck that forever best friends shit. It was on now.

"You have all of two minutes to speak your peace that explains your real reason for being here before I have you removed," I told him, shaking.

"By who?" he challenged me, smiling. "Neil's at a pub watching a game while his girlfriend is enjoying the town with Cookie, PJ and Paige," he replied nastily before snatching my cell out of my hand.

"Desmond McBride! You give me back my cell!" I screamed when the door opened forcefully. When it did, I jumped back, totally scared out of my damn mind.

"Noel, love. You left something," Knight said with a smile that wasn't the kind of smile that said he was happy. "Your clutch. Always forgetting things," he said and grinned as he approached Desmond. "Everything okay in here?"

"Listen, right. So check this out," Desmond said, his voice a few octaves lower like he had past puberty twice. This was hilarious, beyond hilarious. "Noel and I have unfinished business. I understand you might have had your little date last night, but as you can see, the date's over."

"Ah, the infamous Desmond," Knight said, grinning as he dragged his hand down his mouth.

That shit was so sexy, too. I squirmed, remembering how he drew his name all over my body and in my pussy with his tongue.

"I think I've heard something about your upcoming nuptials," he revealed, shocking me. "Cassidy Daniels, right? I know her family very well. Her father and I have done business together in the past. Made a shit load of money. In fact, Cassidy used to have such a huge crush on my baby brother, King. I guess when he didn't take that bait, she moved on." I gasped before laughing and covering my mouth.

What were the chances the only man I've ever loved was

standing in front of the man who makes me want to do it again and with him? I guess Desmond knew that, too, as he refused to back down.

"Look, dude, I fucked up, okay? I shouldn't have even gone there with Cassidy, but I'm telling you, Noel's my girl."

"I am no such thing! Knight, it's not true. How dare you! How dare you pull this stunt after you betrayed me? After you decided to screw things up for us!"

"I didn't try to! Damn, Noel. She's pregnant, alright? Fucking pregnant, and God knows I wish it was you," he said as Knight began to laugh. "What the hell is so funny?"

"Look, whoever you are. This is between me and Noel," Desmond said, poking Knight's chest. "Whatever you think you know about Cassidy and I is some fucking publicity stunt because she's pregnant."

"Wow," was all I said and wanted to say. My mind was blown but for once, I realized I had dodged more than a bullet. I dodged a bomb.

"Noel, please," Desmond plead, taking my hand which pissed Knight off.

"Noel. Tell me what you want me to do? Right now, and I'll do it," Knight told me, reaching for me. I could barely breathe but when he looked at me, I exhaled before I snatched my hand away.

"She doesn't have to—"

"Shut up, Desmond. Just shut up. I can't...I can't, ugh. I'm trying to think, please," I finally got out as Knight's face frowned. I knew Desmond wasn't good for me, but we had history. Then there was Knight, someone I'd met this past week who had been nothing but kind and more than I could have ever imagined. But what if it was just for now, for the moment? I wasn't sure as the air felt thin and I was lightheaded, looking at the both of them.

"Nollie, I'll fix it. I will tell Cassidy it's over, break off the engagement, too. Even tell her to get rid of it," he said with desperation in his voice, and then it was simple. What *it*? Was he calling his child an *it*? Ugh, how did I not see this man was reckless, evil, and selfish?

"Noel, baby. I—I wanted to tell you why I just couldn't cut her off. I mean, even before the baby," he added as if any of what he said was justifying. "See, her father is umm...my new boss."

"Oh, this crap just gets better and better," I replied facetiously, taking a deep breath while Knight stood there fuming. I knew it was fucked up for him to have to witness this, but this was necessary. I had to figure this shit out and fast. "So you mean to tell me that you threw more than ten years of us away for a damn job, Desmond? A job!"

"Now wait a minute, I need that job, Noel. I put in the work, got that damn degree, and I deserve it. I did it not only for me, baby. Can't you see, I did it for us," this lunatic said, eyeing me with his version of love in his eyes. "I want to finally give you a shot to do something *you* want to do. Aren't you tired of slaving at that damn pet store? Making bullshit money just so they can tell you to be grateful? How much are you making a year, Noel? Twenty, maybe thirty thousand and still living at home?"

Oh, he was really letting it all hang out, but who was I to stop him? He was on a roll now.

"I'm working for Mercedes-Benz in the IT department making seventy-five thousand a year and more with patents, Noel? Patents!" he said excitedly while Knight stood there, breathing erratically. I couldn't think. I couldn't fucking think. Not when he was staring at me, pleading with me to give him the light to toss Desmond out of there. I knew it, I could feel it.

"Noel, just don't let this...shit, I guess drug dealer mislead you. I saw the truck, the clothes, the watch he's rocking. Yeah, I see it. Don't fall for it, Noel," he spat, looking at Knight with disgust. "You want to be some prison or sister wife?" he chuckled, as Knight's patience grew thinner as he grunted. He then smiled before he dragged one hand down his face as the smile disappeared.

"I'm out, Noel. It's been real, Noel love," he told me. I moved too slow. I didn't choose him. He was done. Done with me. I'd fucked up royally.

"Exactly! See, he isn't man enough to stand here and tell me I'm wrong. Probably has a lawyer on retainer or some dirty cops on the books. Or...or, I don't know, two or three baby mamas."

"No, Knight. Stop it, just stop," I demanded and grabbed on tightly to his hand.

"Noel..."

"No," I said firmly, shocking him. Hell, shocking me, too. I guess I did have a voice when it mattered. "We just agreed this is what *we* were doing."

"And what is that?" he sneered, looking Desmond's way. "The fuck if I know. Shit, it's only been a few days, right? Nothing major like years of friendship...and lies," he slid in with clenched fists while Neil grunted.

"I don't need years of that to know what we experienced was way more significant, Knight. Listen to me, I choose *you.*"

"This is some nonsense, Nollie," Desmond scoffed, but trust me, his ass was panicking. "Knight's right. A few days is nothing. He's nothing." And when he said that, you could hear a pin drop on cotton with rats tap dancing on it since the tension was so thick.

"Noel, love. Go to my place, now," he said, his voice even tempered, yet his eyes were dark.

"Wait, what?"

"My place, now, Noel, and don't make me repeat myself." Damn it if that man didn't make me feel as if I didn't just have a full body orgasm.

"Okay, just don't be too long," I told him. I refused to look Desmond's way when he called out for me when I walked out the door. The walk wasn't long, but it felt long enough. I knew Desmond deserved everything coming his way, I just prayed Knight used his head. Desmond could be petty and have the cops up here or something. I didn't think for one second he sold drugs, but I knew one thing. That money Desmond was speaking of didn't faze Knight at all.

No more than five minutes later, Knight came inside, and he was pissed. I get it, but I hadn't invited Desmond over. He had to have known that after the night we had. I didn't want another man to touch me if it wasn't Knight.

"So that's Desmond?" he asked, sighing and taking a seat next to me. I flinched as he grabbed my feet. "Noel, don't," he told me firmly. "I'm mad, but I would never hurt you. I also wouldn't touch you *to hurt you*," he told me as his hands rubbed up and down my leg as he rested it on his lap. "You believe me?"

"I do."

"Good, love. First things first, I'm no drug dealer. I know there are things we still need to discuss like our fucking life back home, and we will, but unlike him, I wouldn't dare use money as an incentive to get you and keep you. And keeping it real, the money I have spent on you is nothing in comparison to what I can and will spend on you just for being you. I don't care where you work...wait," he said and paused, dropping his head and laughing.

"You can't be on no pole action or selling pussy. I forgot how you got on that stage and mesmerized my ass. Had me dancing like it was prom and shit. I bet your ass won and we didn't even stay to find out, either. Yeah, I was fucking up. I never leave money on the table," the nut said when I popped his hand.

"What, you got some other talents than the ones I know about?" he shot back with deep knitted brows, scooting away from me.

"Knight, please. Have you seen my body? Can you imagine men paying to see a woman with small portions of tits and ass," I joked, but I saw he didn't take it too kindly when I spoke what he perceived as ill of myself, although I really was joking,

"Don't do that, Noel love. Don't water yourself down because that bitch nigga dragged you or you may not be prissy like the next bitch. That shit is superficial anyway. Trust me, if you are dealing with Knight Commodore, you earned that spot. And you better make sure I earned mine," he spoke with conviction, lifting my chin with his index finger. "Alright?"

"Alright," I groaned, then smiled as he pecked my lips. Then it hit me. "Wait! What happened to Desmond? Knight, don't tell me you did something crazy."

"Let's just say he understands that I can do more damage, like making sure no one in Jonestown, or fuck it, anywhere he lay his head, will ever give him a job."

"Wait, you stay in Jonestown too?"

"Yeah," he admitted with a grin. "Now stay focus with your forgetful ass," this fool told me as I rolled my eyes. "Like I was saying. My name has reach, Noel love. But for you, I won't. I respect he came and tried to fight for you. I respect even more you chose me, but I know the heart. It's stubborn and the love you have for a man after all of that time just doesn't go away."

"I love him, but only as a friend."

"Hey, trust me. I'm no love expert, but I know a few things about the heart. Especially when the heart becomes cold." I could tell that meant more than what we were talking about, too, as he sat back and closed his eyes.

"Wait a minute," I whispered. "Do we have another problem? Like you and a woman?" I asked him, sitting up when he looked at me like I was crazy. "Oh, God. I didn't even ask. I'm such a fool. Such a fool." The entire time I rambled on, this man was laughing.

"You know you are crazy as hell, Noel. First, I had to stand there and watch you and your boyfriend fight hard not to make googly eyes at each other while he tried to downplay some major shit in his life. Then I had to check his ass for even trying you like that and then trying me. You think I really did that for me to hide a whole damn woman, Noel?"

"I...I..."

"You know what, my bad. It is a woman. Her name's Cleo. She's my mother, a fucking alcoholic nut case that ain't did shit for me most of my life, but you know what, Noel? Coming here and being with you really made me feel all kinds of shit I didn't even know existed. And for the first time, I wanted to be able to tell more than just my sister and brother about a girl. I realized that I wanted to tell my mother."

When he did, I could have sworn his eyes became misty as he dropped his head in shame. I wasn't sure what that was about, but until he was ready to share more, I wasn't going to push it. After a few moments of silence, I decided it was time I gave him some time. Hell, I needed it. Even if I was done with Desmond. These few days had been a lot.

"I think I should uh... go," I said, easing up. And when he said nothing nor did he even try to stop me, I knew I was right. I needed to go and he needed to see about his mother.

Damn it, Noel. You're messing up again.

18

KNIGHT COMMODORE

It had been a week since I'd last seen Noel. I wasn't trying to bleed on her with my past bullshit and after I saw what Desmond had done, I knew it was now or never. Cleo and I needed to sit down and finally talk before I fucked things up with Noel. King brought her up, and instead of me going back to my cabin, I chilled with my mother. It was tough the first day, but once she dropped some hot shit on me about things in her past that made her love my father so hard, I got it. I fucking got it.

Today it was Christmas, and for the first time in twenty years, we were all together as a family. I wanted to link up with Noel so bad, but she needed some time away from me, too. We sort of stumbled into each other's lives on some random paths crossing type shit, but damn it if she didn't leave a lasting impression.

I wasn't sweating the distance, though. Noel was mine. I was sure of that. Just when and how that played out, only time could tell. I even had one talk with Rayelle, a final talk, and released that bitch from my life. I couldn't have any drama once I made Noel mine, so Rayelle understood the ramifications of fucking with me. Especially once I really learned how everything went down.

Come to find out, while we felt Rayelle and my mother were in cahoots together for reasons only the two of them would know about, Cleo was making quiet moves that converted into a major outcome. All this time, Rayelle thought she was running the show, it was my mother that was setting Rayelle up. She knew all along about her and Stephen. Even had her proof about a few other men, as well.

Rayelle was so bold, she even tried to pay my mother to leave Jonestown and never return, praying that would push me further into her arms. She figured I would break down sooner or later and wife her once Cleo was gone for good. Did my mother fuck me up in the head and make me not want to love? Hell yeah. But I only got one mother. So I prayed and asked God to give me strength to give her one day to tell that little boy in me anything I needed to know so I could be more than a successful businessman. I wanted to be a better man, *period.* Noel deserved that and I wanted to be that for her.

Surprisingly, the money she had been accepting from Rayelle was going to be used to start a foundation for single mothers with mental health and substance abuse issues. We were calling it *Cleo's Haven of Love.* I told my damn mother she didn't have to steal shit from me since I would have gladly paid for that until she told me I was lying.

She was right, I was. No way before Noel would I even have an open my mind to seek understanding from my mother. Noel made me want to just let go and not always be in control, to just go with the flow and enjoy the ride.

I wanted to do that with my three girls—Queen, Cleo and now Noel. I was even thinking about taking some time off from work to reflect and maybe even volunteer in the community. I gave back with a check, but I wanted to give back by being present with people, hearing their stories, then sowing seeds into their lives.

In the meantime, I did ensure that Queen sent Rayelle a lofty severance package. Even suggested that we wouldn't press charges if she connected with Miss Janice, our former foster mother, and other foster parents to raise money to recruit and pay them an adequate salary for allowing broken children into their home. Miss Janice was cool. Even Mr. George, her husband even though that fool used to look at me like I was fucking his wife.

I just hope Rayelle knew I was serious if she didn't take that money and do as she was told to do. She was a hustler, too, so she could still reap the benefits of fucking with Knight Commodore. She just couldn't fuck me on any level. Especially not this dick. It had an owner. The owner's name was Noel.

On Christmas Eve, we sat around and opened up one gift, but when they opened up mine this morning, they saw an empty box. The empty box was symbolic of the things we wanted to pour into our lives from each other. We each would write them on slips of paper and then open them next Christmas. It was something Miss Reynolds used to have me do. Well, try, but you know what I mean.

Maybe, just maybe my shit took so long just so I could get to where I am today with my family. I even told them that family counseling was a must, reaching out to Miss Reynolds to see if that was something she could do.

I heard she was still practicing in a neighboring small town after retiring from the state. I prayed my small charitable donation to her private practice could change her life or anyone else she chose to bless when she received that one hundred thousand dollar check.

"I have something to say to Knight, if you all don't mind," my mother said, taking a deep breath as the table grew quiet. I could hear the hesitance, the shakiness in her voice, and it was fucking me up. It was never my desire to hate my mother, but I didn't know how to love on her either since she'd stopped teaching me.

Yet and still, she was the only mother I would ever have, and the only one I would ever want.

"Mama," I said, feeling my chest constrict. I guess

because I hadn't called her that since I was maybe nine. Not sure to be honest. "It's okay. You don't have to," I assured her, yet unsure if I could handle what she wanted to share.

Having her there was step two since step one was telling Queen that I'd forgiven her. And Queen, like she always does, pushed the gas on us getting together. She immediately coordinated with King to bring Mama up to Mason and we were now all in the same room amicably.

"No, no, Knight. Let me do this, baby. Let me get it out or I won't be able to sit here and feel like I deserve to be here," she said. Queen, who sat on her right, took her hand and rubbed the top of it as she took a deep breath. King, who sat to Mama's left, leaned up and kissed her cheek.

"It's okay, mama. Everyone one here loves you. Everyone here is family. We got this," I added while I pushed the food around my plate, scared to open my mouth. I did love her, I just didn't trust telling her.

"Knight, I lost myself the day your father died. I mean lost my identity because God knows all I ever wanted to be was his wife and then your mother. I was fine doing just that, even while fighting my own demons inside of me. I felt like I was cursed. I had to be since your father left you three behind who were from him but you weren't him. And while that *should* have been enough, unfortunately, it wasn't. I'm ashamed."

"Mama, don't be," Queen whispered while her eyes met mine across the table. I couldn't fault Queen for being so understanding. Queen was Queen. I sheltered her from the bullshit, so her lens was a little different.

"One thing about love, Knight, and you listen to your mama, you hear. Love is like a drug. It makes you feel like you can do anything. I mean anything. And when you do, you just want more of it. That's how I ended up with you three."

"Uh, mama. I think that's because you and daddy was... you know," King chimed in, as she popped the back of his head.

"Oh, hush up. You was the one that gave me the hardest time," she teased. "You couldn't stand when Knight or Queen got attention."

"He still can't," Queen mumbled, while King told Malachi to get his wife. Malachi wasn't saying shit. He was soaking in the message as he sat Mallory and MJ on his lap, kissing them on the top of their heads.

"And when that love was gone, Knight, I didn't know how to adapt. I let you down, baby. I made you do things like robbing and stealing, and then when they took you all away from me, the little love I had left was depleted," she said, reaching for a napkin from King to dab her eyes. "I started those meetings, you know, and they helped, but what woke me up is a dream. Your father came to me and told me that I better get myself together and get our babies back. I did, but Knight, when I could never get that love from you, I started to give up. Then I decided to just stay out of your way.

At least we could live in the same house and I got a chance to see you. You wouldn't even bring your little friends by, but if I had me for a mother, I probably wouldn't have either."

"Mama, Knight's mean as hell. He ain't have no friends no way," King told her, which made me holler.

"Not true, mama," I offered, trying to offer her a little mercy. "I had a few. Just none worth bringing home. Besides, I had Queen and King. I didn't need friends."

"And for that, I thank you. You kept the family together, and when I told them people at them meetings who my son was, they didn't believe me at first. I wasn't telling them to show off. I was telling them because I was proud. I am honored to be your mother, Knight Easton Commodore."

"Thank you, mama," was all I said. Shit, it was all I could say since we were all barely hanging on, sniffles heard throughout the room.

"Well, thank you, baby. Now, time for Mama to be in your business," she eased in as she sat down. "Someone told me you recently found a young lady that's cute as a button," she said, chuckling as she looked at Queen. I swear that damn Queen talked too much sometimes, but I smiled. Wasn't even conscience that I had until my mouth expressed it.

"Oh, I see that got a little smile out of you. Yes, that is the one, Knight. And while my method to get rid of Rayelle sent you red flags about me, I was glad to prove I hadn't spent a dime. Yes, that girl that has you smiling is the one for you. I see you over there blushing and biting your lip, so I won't dig too deep just yet. The smile says enough for now. Now, let's eat!"

The head of the Commodore family had spoken. After dinner, we sat around the tree and opened up gifts, drank hot cocoa and sang Christmas songs. We even did a little karaoke.

"Hang all the mistle toe, I'm going to get to know you betttter!" Queen sang in the most hideous voice. "This Christmas! And as we trim the tree, how much fun it's gonna be together, this Christmas! The fireside is blazing brighttttt, wow!"

"Wow is right!" King belted and I hollered so hard, clutching my stomach. I hadn't laughed that hard in years, or maybe never. I don't know, but it did feel really good.

By the time Queen was done and Malachi threatened to kill us if we laughed at his kids who sung "Silent Night" by the Temptation, I silently wished they would hurry up. I was tired, but they wouldn't allow me to leave until King and Racha sang, "Santa Baby" by Eartha Kitt. I must have yawned the entire performance when Mallory told Queen someone was outside.

"Oh, that's for me!" Queen shouted excitedly as she hopped up and ran to the door.

"Dude, your wife is so damn friendly. Who could she have met in Mason that would be stopping by?" King asked.

I'd been staying at Queen's to give myself time to

handle things with my mother, but I was missing Noel something serious. I was hoping this wasn't some bitch that she wanted to link me up with after telling Mama about Noel.

"Everyone," Queen sang, getting everyone's attention. "This is Noel Lancaster. A very good friend of Knight's that wanted to stop by and say Merry Christmas.

All I heard, honestly, was "everyone", because after that, nothing else but Noel standing there mattered. She was about to make my third leg stand up too, showing off her thin, yet shapely hips and ass wearing skinny black jeans and guess what? Her wheat-colored Timberland boots. My baby was so fucking sexy, I wanted to peel her clothes off right there and have her for dessert. Especially when she pulled off her peacock coat that revealed a form fitting, cream glittered sweater that hugged her small torso.

"Hey. Good evening, everyone," she said nervously as I stood slowly, wondering how much longer I could before I tackled her. I wanted to slob Noel's little ass down. Love on her, taste her, feel her lips against mine.

"She is adorable," I heard my mother coo.

"As, uh, Queen was saying, I just wanted to stop by and say Merry Christmas. Then I will be out of your way."

Out of my way? What the fuck? Noel was tripping if she thought I was letting her out of my sight now. She knew it, too, as I started walking towards her, causing those eyes to blink. I swear she had blinking condition.

"Knight," she said as I stood in front of her, waiting for her to greet me properly.

"You already know what I want, Noel love," I whispered to where only she could hear me. "Give me some love, love." And like the good girl she was, she lifted up on the balls of her feet and pecked me nice and slow. I had to keep it rated G with Mallory and MJ in here. They were as in tune as Paige and PJ, but they were close by when I heard Mallory say "yuck".

"Can I speak now?" she asked me as I latched on to her waist.

"Alright," was all I said, but I wasn't letting her go. She was going to say whatever the hell she needed to say with my arm wrapped around her body.

"And hello to you, Miss Noel. My son is rude, but I heard he's getting better," my mother said, walking up to Noel and giving her a hug. Well, a side hug because again, I wasn't letting Noel go. "And smiling, too."

"Yeah, I do call him Smiley," she said sneakily while I shot her a look that shut her up.

"Speak, child, before my son has you standing there all day. And don't let him bully you now. It's my first time meeting a girl."

I must have looked like a bashful teenage boy when she did, but I was glad I'd finally introduced a girl to my mother. I can't believe it after all of these years.

"Oh no, Mrs. Commodore. I came without him knowing.

Sort of last minute, but I just wanted to show my appreciation to Knight," she said, waving my mother's warning off. "Then I will be out of your way."

"Word?" I said. I would appreciate some more pussy, but I guess the speech would have to do. "What's in the envelope?" I finally asked her, staring at her suspiciously as Queen egged her own.

"Oh," she said, laughing nervously. "I didn't plan to open it. It's for you to open like later."

I took it from her, and before she knew it, I'd lifted her and took her to the room I'd been sleeping in over there. Yes, Queen had tricked me into staying with all of them in one cabin and I agreed as long as my room was on the opposite side, away from everyone else.

"Knight, we can't be in here alone," she told me in a panic after I tossed her little ass on the bed.

"Why? I'm a grown man and you're a grown woman."

"Who just met your mother," she said then smiled. I already knew why. Without telling her, she could tell my mother and I had made amends. "How's it been?" she whispered as I lowered myself on the bed and pulled her into me. With a tug, I loosened her bun and her locs fell a part just how I liked them.

"It's been alright. Scary," I admitted, holding her tighter. "But still alright."

"That's beautiful. You have a beautiful heart, Knight. You show me that more and more everyday," she said to me lovingly as I held back the tears. "And the envelope was really a thank you."

"For?" I asked, never wanting to let her go.

"Paying off my parents' loan," she shared, which made me sigh, shaking my head.

"It was supposed to be anonymous."

"My father insisted that the bank show him the cleared check. So, Commodore Enterprises, huh?"

"You know."

"I know, but it doesn't change anything."

"Oh, yeah? Why not?" I asked, smiling down at her as I played in her hair. "Because that envelope and that freaking money you stuck in my boot after I paid you back, Knight."

I laughed because I did stick that damn money in one of her boots. That was a fucking insult. Once I give you something, it's that—a got damn gift. I laughed because I knew she was determined to pay off her debt, but I could never repay her for fixing my fucked up heart.

"How about you pay off that other debt, your parents' loan, with some pussy," I teased, flipping her over and tickling her until she screamed she was about to pee on herself.

"Knight, please," she groaned, her face flushed as she began to whimper.

"Alright then. No pussy, which was a joke, but there is one more thing you can do," I told her as I settled down, rubbing her back as she sat next to me. "Stay another day... I'm just saying. It's Christmas."

"Only one more day?"

"One day feels like a lifetime anyway, Noel. They all mean the same to me as long as you're with me."

"Hmmm," she teased, with her finger pressed against the side of her chin. She better stop fucking with me as I shot her a look. "I think I might be able to accommodate that request, Smiley," she agreed, calling me that damn name again, but I guess she was right. Since she'd come into my life, I guess I did begin to smile. That's all I wanted to do. That was be with Noel and do more of that smiling shit.

The End

www.ingramcontent.com/pod-product-compliance
Ingram Content Group UK Ltd.
Pitfield, Milton Keynes, MK11 3LW, UK
UKHW022021190726
13853UKWH00005B/2036

9 798523 445682